D1136524

FOR SALE

Ap4

Turbo
Drive

Look out for

TURBO DRIVE

Jonny Zucker

SCHOLASTIC

First published in the UK in 2012 by Scholastic Children's Books
An imprint of Scholastic Ltd
Euston House, 24 Eversholt Street
London, NW1 1DB, UK
Registered office: Westfield Road, Southam, Warwickshire, CV47 0RA
SCHOLASTIC and associated logos are trademarks and/or
registered trademarks of Scholastic Inc.

Text copyright © Jonny Zucker, 2012

The right of Jonny Zucker to be identified as the author
of this work has been asserted by him.

ISBN 978 1 407 12105 5

A CIP catalogue record for this book is available
from the British Library.

All rights reserved.
This book is sold subject to the condition that it shall not,
by way of trade or otherwise, be lent, hired out or otherwise circulated
in any form of binding or cover other than that in which it is published.
No part of this publication may be reproduced, stored in a retrieval system,
or transmitted in any form or by any means (electronic, mechanical,
photocopying, recording or otherwise) without the prior
written permission of Scholastic Limited.

Printed and bound by CPI Group (UK) Ltd, Croydon, CR0 4YY
Papers used by Scholastic Children's Books are made from
wood grown in sustainable forests.

1 3 5 7 9 10 8 6 4 2

This is a work of fiction. Names, characters, places,
incidents and dialogues are products of the author's imagination
or are used fictitiously. Any resemblance to actual people, living or dead,
events or locales is entirely coincidental.

www.scholastic.co.uk/zone

For Jake, Ben and Isaac

COVENTRY CITY LIBRARIES	
3 8002 01984 4259	
PETERS	15-Feb-2012
JF	£5.99
APL GM	27·2·12

The kart flew round a corner, its blue sidebars a blurred flash of colour to the spectators surrounding the track. It was a "Demo Sunday" at Sparks Cross Karting Club and Danny Sharp was going for broke.

Sparks Cross was Danny's home turf – he knew every single inch of the track. The course at 1100 metres long, was a slightly off-kilter figure of eight with four straights and six bends.

The kart's slick tyres pounded the tarmac as he came off the bend. Danny was in pole position – he'd left the other nine drivers in his wake at the end of the fourth lap and this was the sixth, and final one. His nearest competitor was over fifty metres behind him.

At sixty-five mph – the maximum speed of the kart – Danny shot down the second to last straight, the wind zipping by the vehicle. In his chest burned the familiar feeling of exhilaration and excitement – the same intoxicating mix he experienced whenever he was out on the track. Computer games and basketball were great but this was where he most wanted to be.

A momentary pang passed through Danny as he thought about what had happened to his own kart. It had been a Christmas present from his parents – his pride and joy. It was second-hand but in excellent condition – a real beauty. It had seen him through many practice and race days but to Danny's horror, it had been smashed up six weeks ago. It had been in the club's kart shed and one night someone had laid waste to it.

His dad's friend Spike owned a kart repair shop, and he had got the kart into decent enough shape for one last race – the Granger Cup Quarter-Final. Danny had made it through that race and qualified for the semis, but since then the kart had been languishing in his back yard – broken and defeated.

Danny was pretty sure he knew who had wrecked it.

Forget all of that, Danny ordered himself. *Just keep your mind on the track and steer clear of danger.*

This principle had been drummed into him from the moment he'd climbed into a kart. All you had to do was mention the name Ayrton Senna and a chill passed through Danny. Senna – the Brazilian maestro – had crashed and died in a Formula One race. The tragedy still cast a shadow over the entire racing world.

Some people scoffed at the rigorous safety checks involved with driving nowadays, but an accident was always potentially a split second away if you didn't keep on high alert. The ambulance that stood beside the Sparks Cross track was testament to the very real dangers associated with the sport. There had even been an air ambulance here a couple of years back, after a kart had flipped over, but thankfully the boy who'd crashed had been incredibly lucky and had managed to escape with just bad bruising.

Danny hit the home straight and took the middle of

the track, sweeping over the finishing line. He braked and quickly brought the kart's speed down, steering it into the start/finish area. He killed the kart's power, undid the seat straps and hoisted himself out of the vehicle. A large group of children and teenagers, and an assortment of adults, applauded him heartily.

"And that was only a demonstration race!" laughed Alfie Price, walking over and giving Danny a slap on the back.

Alfie owned Sparks Cross. He was Danny's karting mentor and at just over six feet tall, Alfie was a commanding presence. He had silver hair, royal blue eyes and an L-shaped scar on his left cheek. The scar and the slight limp Alfie walked with were the only signs of the terrible accident he'd suffered when he was eighteen. Alfie's leg had been smashed up badly enough to end any prospects he had of a racing career, but he wasn't bitter about it; far from it

Danny took off his helmet and grinned. He loved Demo Sundays, when non-members were invited to Sparks Cross to take a closer look and see if they fancied joining up.

"OK, everyone," said Alfie, walking off the track to a large patch of grass with Danny at his side. The spectators gathered round. "This Demo Day is part of a national initiative called *Get Karting*. The idea is that on days such as these, loads of children and young people get to try out kart driving."

The visitors looked up at Alfie with nerves and excitement.

"Here at Sparks Cross we're looking for enthusiastic young drivers who are willing to dedicate several weekends a year to the club and to racing," continued Alfie. "We deliberately keep costs down to a minimum because we don't want to exclude anyone. We have to charge something to keep the club going, but we always stress that absolutely everyone is welcome, regardless of their financial situation."

There were several nods from approving parents. Alfie was always good at making people feel included.

"Danny Sharp here is one of our best drivers. He joined the club at seven and has been here ever since. I have very big hopes for him."

Danny felt his cheeks redden slightly.

"I hope watching Danny and the other drivers has inspired some of you to join us. Obviously, as for most of you it will be your first time behind the wheel, we encourage you to take it easy. But even at twenty miles per hour you can experience some of the thrill associated with the sport. The actual driving sessions will begin in half an hour and as you've all registered and paid your day fee, I'm going to draw up a schedule. While I'm off doing that, I'd like you to have the opportunity to ask a couple of drivers any questions you may have about karts and karting, starting with Danny here. Who'd like to go first?"

"Have you ever been injured?" asked a boy of about ten.

Before Danny replied, Alfie winked at him and then headed off in the direction of the clubhouse.

Danny turned to the asker of the question. Boys often asked this question, hoping to hear some gory details. Unfortunately this kid was in for a disappointment.

"Just cuts and bruises," replied Danny, "but so far, thankfully, nothing serious."

"How often do you race?" asked a bright-eyed girl of eight.

"Generally it's every couple of weeks, although sometimes it's more often. Over a racing weekend, Saturday is practice day and Sunday is race day. You generally do six laps each time you're out there."

"Do you have to wear special clothes?" asked a sulky-looking girl about Danny's age.

"Yeah," nodded Danny. "For a start, you need a racing suit." He indicated his blue suit. "It's lightweight but protective. You also need to wear specialized karting boots, like these ones. Plus you need a rib protector."

"A rib protector?" asked the girl, "Why? You're not having a fight out there, are you?"

Some of the kids laughed and Danny joined in. "There's no fighting," he smiled, "but when you take the corners, the pressure on your ribs is really intense. The sheer force could easily break them. That's why you have the protector. You can still get bruises on your ribs, but to date, I've not broken any of them."

"Who is your F1 hero?" asked one of the dads.

"Scot Devlin," answered Danny.

"But he's relatively new on the block, isn't he?" said the dad.

"He's fairly new," nodded Danny, "but he's fifth on the leader board and in my view he has everything: strength, steering ability, bravery, flexibility. I think he's the man for the next few years."

What Danny didn't mention was that he'd actually met Devlin on several occasions and that Devlin had said Danny reminded him of himself at the same age! Danny could still hardly believe these meetings had happened.

Danny took a few more questions, and as he was answering one about the various driving categories, he caught a glimpse of a tall and stocky man having a word with Danny's dad before getting into a silver Range Rover and driving off. The man was Mr Frank Hoult – managing director of Point Power Electronics and a potential sponsor of Danny's. Danny and Dad were meeting him tomorrow. Mr Hoult might represent the difference between a future in driving or early retirement.

"OK, that's enough questions for Danny," said one of the stewards helping Alfie out for the day. "You can ask more questions to the driver who finished second."

Danny's gaze was diverted away from the silver Range

Rover to the driver who had come in second and was waiting by the trackside: Tony Butler.

Tony was a boasting, vain wind-up merchant, who'd been in Danny's class throughout primary school, was in his form group at secondary school and had recently become a member at Sparks Cross; Tony would also be racing in next Sunday's Granger Cup Semi-Final with Danny.

In the quarter-final Tony had deliberately driven his kart into the side of Danny's, nearly causing a serious crash. With a huge amount of strength and skill, Danny had managed to pull his kart back under control and grab second place, while pushing Tony back into third. There'd been a judicial after the race but Tony's insistence that it was an "accident" had somehow convinced the race clerk and Tony had got the go-ahead to race in the semis.

But worse than any of that was the fact that Danny was certain it had been Tony who'd smashed up his kart. He had no proof but he also had no doubt.

Tony started lecturing the gathered spectators about how amazing his orange kart was. The black stripes on its side pods, the sparkling axles and the intricate purple patterns on its nose cone and rear bar made it really stand out.

"It's got a fantastic 125cc two-stroke water-cooled engine," Tony was saying as loud as he could; loud enough for Danny to hear every boastful word. "It does nought to sixty in three seconds and can do seventy miles per hour easy."

When Tony had finished his question-and-answer session, the crowd moved on to the clubhouse to find out the schedule for their driving sessions.

Tony sauntered over to Danny as if *he* were the owner of Sparks Cross, not Alfie.

"So you'll be driving one of the rubbish club karts in the semis," sneered Tony, his over-gelled hair resting greasily on his head.

"I would have been driving *my own* kart if it hadn't smashed it up by some idiot!" hissed Danny furiously.

"What are you trying to say?" demanded Tony, shoving his face a few centimetres away from Danny's.

"You know exactly what I'm saying!" snapped Danny. "I'm looking at the culprit!"

"Produce some proof before you go making accusations!" Tony laughed nastily. "I'm definitely going to prove I'm better than you in the semi-final!" he sneered over his shoulder as he walked away, still laughing.

"We'll see!" shouted Danny after him. "We'll . . . see!"

"This suit is so uncomfortable it feels like it's got itching powder inside!" complained Danny.

Danny nerve endings jangled.

His hands were clammy.

His teeth were gritted.

But he wasn't out on the track.

He and his dad had just entered a large black-tiled reception area of a seven-storey glass-fronted building. At the far end of a vast reception area was a large chrome desk. The words POINT POWER ELECTRONICS were emblazoned high on the wall above the desk and giant photos of company products adorned the other walls – drills and saws and workstations.

Point Power Electronics had initially rebuffed Dad's request for sponsorship. However, soon after their rejection letter had been despatched, a new managing director called Frank Hoult had joined the company. He'd come across the letter, read what Dad had to say about Danny's karting career to date and aspirations for the future and had invited them both in.

Despite money being tight in the Sharp household, Dad had insisted on buying Danny a grey suit and tie for the meeting. Danny would have far preferred to wear jeans and a hoodie, but he knew in his heart that Dad was right; he needed to make a good impression – show Mr Hoult he was serious. Dad was also wearing a suit – the black one he wore for funerals.

Dad smoothed a hand through his hair.

"You haven't got enough hair to worry about!" hissed Danny.

Dad grinned and together they approached the reception desk. A man in a blue jacket looked up.

"The Sharps to see Mr Hoult," said Dad.

The man checked his appointments log, issued them with security badges and told them to take the lift to the seventh floor.

They did so and walked down a wide corridor, stopping at another reception desk. Behind this one sat a petite woman with long red hair and high cheekbones who wore a badge stating "Angie Kelly".

"Ed and Danny Sharp," said Dad.

"Hi," replied Angie, "I'm Mr Hoult's personal assistant. Please take a seat and he'll see you shortly."

They sat on two leather armchairs. Dad picked up a company catalogue. Danny's feet tapped out a rhythm on the parquet flooring. He was nervous, more nervous than he'd been in the Granger Cup Quarter-Final. What happened in the meeting he was about to enter could change the course of his life. If Mr Hoult agreed to sponsor him, it might mean opening the door to an eventual arrival in Formula One – Danny's all-time dream. A no would be devastating.

Danny's fingers drummed on the armrests. Dad gave him an encouraging pat on the back. And then the phone on Angie's desk rang. She took the call and quickly replaced the handset.

"Mr Hoult will see you now," she announced and opened a large oak door just to the right of her desk.

"Thanks," Dad said as he and Danny entered and found themselves in a spacious office with sunshine streaming through huge windows and a large walnut desk at one end.

Frank Hoult dragged his eyes away from a tiny silver laptop, stood up and leant across his desk to shake Danny and Dad's hands.

Up close, Mr Hoult had a ruddy face, dark brown eyes and a thick moustache. He looked a bit like an affable farmer in a Sunday night TV series.

"Sorry I didn't get to talk to you at the Demo Day yesterday, Danny," said Mr Hoult, "but I did manage to say hello to your dad."

"No problem," replied Danny nervously.

"Good," smiled Mr Hoult. "Thanks very much for coming in to see me. Please make yourselves comfortable." He indicated the two chairs facing his desk.

They sat, Danny's heart rattling around his chest like an out of control basketball.

"As you know," said Mr Hoult, "soon after joining this company I took a look at Point Power's work in the community and I realized there was very little going on. I searched through the file, found the rejection letter we sent to you and decided it might be something I was interested in. I'm a very big fan of Formula One and get to at least two Grand Prix a year. I also loved karting as a boy, but I didn't get anywhere near your level, Danny. As agreed in our subsequent correspondence, I came to watch you on the track at Sparks Cross yesterday, and I was impressed with what I saw."

Danny felt a pang of hope in his chest.

"How often do you manage to get down to the track?" asked Mr Hoult.

"Three, sometimes four times a week," replied Danny. "If it wasn't for schoolwork I'd be there twenty-four/seven."

"I'm glad to hear you're aware of both," nodded Mr Hoult, "a dedication to driving and a commitment to keep up with your schoolwork."

"His school reports are good," cut in Dad. "He always

does his homework and gets his projects in on time."

Mr Hoult spread out his palms and placed them flat on his desk. "OK," he said, "let's get down to business."

Danny's nerves fizzed wildly.

"First of all, I have to make it clear that here and now I can't make either of you any promises. Enjoying watching you race is one thing, Danny; sponsoring you is something quite different."

A judder of disappointment hit Danny's throat.

"If I do decide that backing you is a good idea, I'd have to convince an awful lot of people here that it's the right thing to do. Yes, I firmly believe in doing work for and with the community, but if Point Power were to sponsor you, it would only be worth doing if we get something back."

"You mean money?" asked Danny.

"Money would certainly be part of it," nodded Mr Hoult. "Not necessarily right now, but we'd have to be pretty sure that we have a strong chance of making some financial gain from your driving in the future. For us to achieve that you'd need to be very successful. Do you have it in you to be very successful, Danny?"

Danny swallowed nervously. "Making it in Formula One is what I've wanted to do for as long as I can remember. I'm totally focused on driving and I'm totally determined to make it up through the ranks."

"You've seen his track record," pointed out Dad. "Seventeen cups, hundreds of race wins."

Mr Hoult nodded. "If we got behind you and your career *did* take off, of course we'd also gain from our association with you. It could be a feather in the Point Power Electronics cap."

"If you back me I won't let you down," said Danny, "I'd do everything I could to get better and better as a driver. I promise you."

"I believe you," replied Mr Hoult, "but unfortunately in life, some promises are impossible to keep."

"He has an excellent attitude," said Dad quickly, "and his mum and I will support him all of the way."

"If I don't have a company like you behind me, there's no way I'll ever make it," said Danny. "My dad's a postman, my mum's a bookkeeper. I'm not criticizing those jobs, I'm just saying we're never going to be ultra-rich like some of the other families on the circuit.

I could never afford to progress without sponsorship."

"You're right," agreed Mr Hoult. "Racing is becoming more of a chequebook sport every day. That punishes parents with lesser means, however hard they work. It's not right and as someone who grew up in a household with very little money, I know exactly how that feels."

Danny nodded earnestly. This was positive, wasn't it?

Silence hung in the air for several moments. Danny sat forward in his chair as he felt the tension ratchet up several notches.

Mr Hoult was the one who broke the silence. "And your next race is the Granger Cup Semi-Final on Sunday?"

Danny nodded but at that second Mr Hoult's phone rang. He picked it up briskly.

Danny and Dad heard Angie's tinny voice tell him that his next appointment had arrived.

Mr Hoult replaced the receiver. "Sorry," he smiled, "there's a lot of pressure on my time at the moment, so we'll have to end it there."

"We understand," replied Dad.

"I genuinely think you have potential, Danny," said

Mr Hoult, eyeing them both seriously. "I know I've only seen you drive six laps, but that was enough to show me that the talent and skill is there. Like I said, though, at this stage, I can't promise you anything. Sponsorship in any form represents a big financial risk for the company."

Danny's shoulders slumped a bit.

"On the positive side, however," Mr Hoult added, "I'm a quick worker and I'm going to talk to several colleagues about this very soon. I don't believe in letting people hang on."

"I don't want to be rude," said Danny, "but do you know what kind of time frame we're talking about here?"

"Well," sighed Mr Hoult, "it just so happens that some budgets have to be set this week, so if anything does happen it will need to be sorted quickly. I'm talking days rather than weeks."

"Really?" asked Danny. He felt his heart lift up again. Talk about a roller coaster ride of hope, dashed expectations and hope again! Point Power could become his sponsor in *days*! If it was a yes and it came before next weekend, there might even be a chance of getting a new kart for the Granger Cup Semi-Final; how excellent would that be! He'd love to see the look on Tony Butler's face if Danny showed up in a state-of-the-art monster kart!

Mr Hoult stood up.

Danny and Dad stood too, and they all shook hands again.

"Angie will be in touch," said Mr Hoult, his eyes already flitting back to his computer screen.

And that was that.

Danny left the office still reeling from the criss-cross of feelings, taking in excitement, despair, hope and fear. After saying goodbye to Angie on Reception, Danny and Dad were soon back out into the Point Power car park.

"I liked him," said Dad, unlocking the doors of his Fiat Doblo. "He seemed like a no-nonsense guy."

The Doblo wasn't exactly a vehicle Danny would have chosen for himself (he'd have gone for a Ferrari 458) but with four cylinders, sixteen valves and 1598 cubic capacity, the Doblo was perfect for Dad, who often carried loads of gear around – mainly the boxes of tools he needed for his part-time work of doing up old-ish cars and selling them on for a profit.

"But do you think he'll say yes?" asked Danny eagerly.

"I have no idea," said Dad, as they both climbed into the van. "On the plus side, he's a big fan of driving and wants to put something back into the community. On the minus side, he is very new to the job and other senior managers could easily dissuade him if they don't think it's best for the company."

Dad switched the ignition key and pulled out of the car park.

"But can you imagine if he says yes," murmured Danny. "I could be driving a brand new, high spec kart in *days*! And we'd keep this one at home all the time, so no one could touch it. I'm not having it smashed up in the Sparks Cross shed like my old one. It'll stay with us except on practice and race days."

"I think we should try and remain calm about this," said Dad, pursing his lips. "The last thing I want is to have you getting your hopes up. It could easily be a no – you have to be prepared for that."

Danny felt a jolt of anger crunch inside his chest. "Don't be so negative, Dad!" he snapped, even though he knew what his father was saying made sense; he just couldn't help it.

"I'm not being negative!" Dad replied calmly. "He was obviously impressed with your progress and your attitude, but until he signs a cheque, nothing's happened."

Danny huffed.

"I just don't want you getting hurt – that's all," said Dad. "I'm trying to protect you!"

"Well I don't need protecting!" snapped Danny, hunching up in his seat.

Dad muttered something under his breath.

Danny scowled and pulled off his itchy suit jacket.

What was it with parents – why couldn't they just let you dream sometimes?

"So let me get this straight: he didn't *promise* anything, but you reckon this Mr Hoult guy *might* come up with the goods?"

Danny and his best friend, Carl, were sitting on a bench next to the basketball courts in the park. The sky was blue with some patchy clouds and a light breeze drifted through the air. It was mid-afternoon and every word of that morning's meeting with Mr Hoult was seared into Danny's brain.

"He said he saw my potential at the Demo Day,"

Danny enthused, "and he wants to put something back into the community."

Carl popped a piece of chewing gum into his mouth and offered one to Danny, who declined. "Well, as your manager, I have to say this is FANTASTIC!" grinned Carl. "It could be the difference between you driving a Ford Fiesta or a Porsche. Think of what our bank balances might look like in the future. If this Mr Hoult comes on board it'll be champagne and holidays to the Bahamas!"

Danny laughed. "My dad gave me the usual speech about not getting my hopes up."

"Parents are programmed to do that," groaned Carl. "They always try to plan for every eventuality; they're so boring!"

"I agree," nodded Danny. "I forgot to say that Mr Hoult said he'd let us know in days rather than weeks."

"Seriously?" mouthed Carl. "I better iron my best clothes for the signing-up ceremony."

Danny cracked up laughing. Carl always had this effect on him.

"Can you believe the summer holidays are almost

over?" groaned Carl a few seconds later, bringing Danny out of racing heaven and back down to earth.

"I know," sighed Danny. "Six weeks of delicious freedom and now just one day before it's back to the slog."

"At least we've got Mr Stewart as our form tutor again," pointed out Carl.

"Yeah, but we only have a couple of lessons together now," countered Danny.

"Before we get overwhelmed by our dread of school, why don't we shoot some hoops?" suggested Carl.

"Definitely!" agreed Danny, brightening up.

Carl grabbed his basketball and stood up. "Me versus you, first to ten baskets wins," he announced, bouncing the ball and running off in the direction of the courts.

"You're on!" shouted Danny, springing to his feet and haring after Carl, desperate to nick the ball off his best mate.

"Here you go, Danny," said Mum, passing him a plate with a large portion of her delicious lasagne on.

"Cheers, Mum," replied Danny, reaching for his fork.

It was seven p.m. on Tuesday. Danny had spent the day getting his stuff ready for the start of school tomorrow.

The Sharp family were sitting down to a meal in the kitchen.

The kitchen had a cosy feel. It was well lived in, but generally pretty tidy apart from when Katie – Danny's six-year-old sister – was doing one of her epic race-driving paintings. Like her big brother, she had the car bug and was counting down the days to her seventh birthday when she'd be allowed to join Sparks Cross and finally get behind the wheel of a kart.

"I've got Mrs Rogers as my teacher this year," said Katie. "She used to be a professional netball player."

Danny and his parents knew this fact well. Katie had told them about ten million times that summer.

"Will they start piling on the work pressure straight away, Danny?" asked Dad, buttering a bread roll and putting it on Katie's plate.

"I hope not," sighed Danny, "the summer exams were bad enough."

"Will you still have time for racing?" asked Katie, suddenly looking worried.

"Of course!" laughed Danny, ruffling her hair. "You're coming to watch me on Sunday, remember?"

"Oh yes!" grinned Katie. "And next year it will be me out there too, won't it?"

"Yeah," grinned Danny, "and it will be me watching you!"

"Brilliant!" squealed Katie.

After the meal, Danny washed the dishes while Dad dried up. Then he went up to his room to check out some karting magazines and listen to some new tunes he'd downloaded. He was barely through the door when his mobile rang.

NUMBER BLOCKED read the display.

Could he be bothered to talk to someone selling carpet cleaners or house insurance? Danny sighed and answered the call.

"Danny, it's Scot Devlin."

Danny nearly dropped his phone.

Scot Devlin – his Formula One hero – on the phone.

"Hi, Scot!"

Just saying his name felt freaky.

"I've been meaning to call you for a while, but things have been pretty hectic round here. How's it going, Danny?"

"Yeah . . . it's good. I was out at Sparks Cross on Sunday, helping out on a Demo Day."

"I remember open days!" laughed Devlin. "Hundreds

of kids desperate to get their hands on a kart with their parents either freaking out about the dangers, or groaning about the kind of money involved!"

Danny laughed, and then he remembered the meeting with Mr Hoult. "Me and my dad met a potential sponsor yesterday too."

"Great!" enthused Devlin. "Who is it and do they have a track record in Formula One?"

"They're called Point Power Electronics," replied Danny. "They've never been involved in sponsoring a driver before, but the managing director is a big F1 fan. He seemed pretty positive."

"Excellent," said Devlin. "Is Sunday the Granger Cup Semi-Final?"

"Yeah," replied Danny, impressed that Devlin had remembered the name of the race.

"Are you ready for it?"

"I don't know. . . Do you ever know if you're ready for a race?"

"The more you drive, the more prepared you get," replied Devlin.

"Do you still get nervous?" asked Danny.

"Of course I do! Come on – there are millions of people all over the world watching every F1 race; if I mess up, it's all there in slow-motion and beautiful high definition for everyone to see!"

Danny laughed and then murmured, "I hope I can make it up to F1 one day."

"Just stay focused and keep driving and you never know," hit back Devlin. "You have to aim high."

"Understood," replied Danny.

"Anyway," Devlin went on, "as well as checking up on my protégé, there's another reason I'm phoning."

Danny's heart zipped around his chest. *He called me his protégé!*

"Tomorrow night I'm doing a product launch for a new watch called the Dawn Thread. It's made by that posh watch company, Saramas; do you know it?"

"Yeah," replied Danny, who'd often seen its sumptuous adverts in the glossy colour supplements of Sunday newspapers.

"How would you like it if I slapped you and a mate on the official guest list for the event? It's at Collinwood, you know, the massive department store in town. Come to the launch and then afterwards, we can hang out a bit, talk about driving and stuff."

"Are you serious?" asked Danny, his eyes widening with excitement.

"Absolutely," replied Devlin, "what do you say?"

"I say yes!" shouted Danny. "I'll bring my best mate Carl – he won't believe it!"

"Excellent! It kicks off at eight thirty. Get there a bit earlier – your names will be on the guest list as Danny Sharp plus one, OK?"

"That's brilliant!" enthused Danny.

"Great!" laughed Devlin. "I'll see you both tomorrow night."

"Fantastic – thanks, Scot."

The call was suddenly over and Danny was sitting on his bed in shock. He stayed there for at least a minute holding his phone and grinning madly to himself. He then let out a roaring cheer of delight that brought his parents and Katie racing into his room.

He quickly told them about the invite and after a bit of negotiating – "It's the night of your first day back at school!" pointed out Mum – Danny got the go-ahead to attend the launch as long as he promised to be home by ten-thirty p.m. at the very latest and go straight to bed when he got in.

Then he speed-dialled Carl to share the news flash.

"Are you winding me up?" asked Carl.

When Danny explained it wasn't a wind-up, he had to wait for Carl to go crazy, tell his parents and get them to agree to the same terms as Danny's parents.

"I'm going to meet Scot Devlin!" trilled Carl. "I better wear some smart clothes. If he's unhappy with his present management do you think he might consider switching his allegiance to me?"

By the time Carl had spent a further ten minutes going over all of the subjects they could talk to Devlin about, Danny felt exhausted.

"I'm hanging up," he told Carl, "I'll see you tomorrow."

"Definitely," sighed Carl happily. "When it comes to me writing my autobiography, I'll note tomorrow night down as the moment that *I* . . . I mean . . . *we* . . . really arrived!"

"I've made Mrs Rogers a welcome card," said Katie proudly, showing Danny her creation, which was covered in karts and Formula One racing cars and a series of netball nets, with Mrs Rogers making an ambitious and impressive pass to a teammate.

"Nice one!" smiled Danny, who was trying to get his head round having to get up early and be ready for school – it was hard after weeks of lie-ins. Dad had left the house at about six a.m. for his postman's shift.

Danny was just finishing up his cereal when the

phone rang. Mum answered it and listened to the caller without saying anything. Then she handed the phone to Danny, saying, "It's Angie from Point Power Electronics."

Danny felt a surge of electricity zing in his body. *Is she phoning to tell me Mr Hoult has agreed to sponsor me?* With hope dancing in his chest he dashed over to take the phone. Mum held her hands up as a way of telling him to calm down before he spoke. He nodded and waited a few seconds.

"Hi, it's Danny here," he began, his whole body tensed with expectation.

"Hi, Danny. I know that Mr Hoult has already seen you on the track but he's asked if you could send us some footage of you driving asap. He'll show this to a group of other people here. He's asked for the footage to include as many aspects of your driving as possible; would that be something you could do?"

"Sure," replied Danny, trying to keep the disappointment from his voice. "I probably can get it to you late afternoon or early evening today."

"That would be great," said Angie. "Here's Mr Hoult's

email address; if you could send it directly to him, that would much appreciated."

Danny grabbed a pen and a scrap of paper and took down the email address.

"Once he's seen the footage, do you have any idea when he'll actually make a decision?" asked Danny.

"Yes," replied Angie. "He said Friday at the latest."

Danny's heart pumped like crazy. Friday! If it was a yes, he really *might* just be able to get a new kart before the Granger Cup Semi-Final!

"Er . . . you don't have any idea of *what* he's going to decide, do you?" he asked, his words laced with anxiety.

"I'm sorry, Danny. I'm not party to those discussions at all," replied Angie. "I know as much as you do. But I've got my fingers crossed for you. Email him the footage and see what happens, OK?"

"Yes. Thanks very much. I'm on it."

He replaced the receiver, his brain working like crazy.

"Mr Hoult wants to see some film of me driving," Danny told his mother.

"Have you got any?"

"Yeah, bits and pieces, but I'll go down to Sparks

Cross after school and get some new stuff. Alfie will help me."

"That's fine," nodded Mum, "but you'll need to come home, have supper and do your homework before you set out for the watch launch. And don't forget, you promised to be back at ten-thirty at the very latest."

Danny had momentarily forgotten about the launch; he and Carl were going to be hanging out with Scot Devlin tonight. That beat a session slumped in front of a quiz show on TV!

Danny set off for school, dreading the start of lessons again but buoyed by the prospect of taking some good footage with Alfie later on. He met Carl by the school gates and told him about Angie's call.

"You need to make that footage blow his mind!" exclaimed Carl. "Make it look like you are the true future of F1. Get the guy to sit up and look at your driving with amazement, and an open wallet, of course!"

Danny laughed and they headed off to their form room for registration.

Danny felt his muscles tighten when Tony Butler entered, but Tony was heavily engrossed in a conversation with his best mate, Kev, so he didn't pay Danny any attention. And the rest of the morning was fine. Tony wasn't in any of Danny's classes. Double English was followed by maths and music, in which the class got to start a composition using Garage Band. Danny and Carl had music together so they worked on a track jointly, using some amazing beats they found on a website.

In the lunch hour, after scoffing their packed lunches in the canteen, they went to check out the new equipment in a room situated next to the school gym. Mr Neale, the head of PE, was a real fitness freak and he'd convinced the powers that be to invest in some rowing and running machines as well as a decent stash of weights. He'd put some posters up around school inviting pupils in to inspect the gear.

"No one is allowed to use any of this equipment unsupervised," announced Mr Neale to a group of students, waving his arm round the room to show off the gear, which looked like it had been unpacked in the last ten minutes: brand new and spotless. "There must ALWAYS be a member of staff present."

"Is that for safety or because he thinks someone will nick his precious gear?" whispered Danny.

Carl grinned.

"I don't want any accidents on mine or anyone else's watch," added Mr Neale. "If handled incorrectly, this gear can cause serious injuries. If you want to use any of it you'll need to book yourself in. The book will be on that shelf over there. I'm restricting it to eight people at any one time. You can have thirty minutes max in here. That way as many people as possible will get to go on the equipment. It'll also be used in some lessons with small groups; the rest of the PE staff have undergone training with it, so they know what they're doing."

Everyone nodded.

Mr Neale then spent twenty minutes demonstrating how each piece of machinery was used. "Tell anyone else who's not here but wants to use this place that they'll also have to watch my equipment demo before they touch anything."

Danny was one of the first to sign up – his upper body strength was reasonable but he needed to build it up. Some people thought motorsport just involved chilling out in a comfortable seat while steering, but you needed every possible ounce of strength if you wanted to race to the best of your ability.

The afternoon was filled with geography and double science, both of which were bearable. As soon as the school day was over, Danny grabbed his bag.

"I'm heading to Sparks Cross to get that footage. What are you up to, Carl?"

They were in a corridor next to the lockers. Streams of kids were chatting, grabbing bags and heading home.

"I've got ICT club," responded Carl. He was a bit of a computer wizard. "I'll give you a bell later to see how it goes with Alfie."

"Top man!" grinned Danny. "Come over to mine at seven forty-five; that'll give us time to get to town in time for the launch."

They exchanged a high five and Danny hurried for the exit, fully aware that the footage he was about to shoot could be the most important piece of film in his entire life.

A twenty-minute bus ride later and Danny was striding down the lane leading to Sparks Cross. Where it had been full to brimming with chattering voices and fascinated eyes on the Demo Day, the place was now deserted. Danny headed straight towards Alfie's office.

"Danny Sharp!" grinned Alfie as Danny walked in.

"Hey, Alfie, how's it going?"

"Not bad at all," replied Alfie, "how was your first day back at school?"

"It was OK," replied Danny, "but much more importantly, on Monday Dad and I met that potential sponsor I told you about."

"The guy from Point Power Electronics?" replied Alfie. "Did he show at the Demo Day?"

Danny nodded. "He's called Frank Hoult. I really wanted him to meet you, but he didn't stay long. He watched me driving, had a quick chat with Dad and then headed off."

"And how did the meeting go?"

"Yeah, it was good. I was really nervous beforehand but Mr Hoult said some positive things about my driving so I managed to relax a bit."

"And the outcome?" asked Alfie expectantly.

"He said he couldn't promise anything and needed to speak to lots of people before he made a decision. He also talked about how Point Power will want a return on their investment if they sponsor me."

"Of course they will," nodded Alfie sagely. "No business ever does something without getting something back. Did he talk about any sort of schedule?"

Danny pursed his lips. "He's going to try and make a decision by Friday at the latest."

"*This* Friday!" cried Alfie.

Danny nodded. "I know, it's all really fast, but there's something to do with budgets that needs sorting quickly."

Alfie patted Danny on the shoulder. "Let's hope Point Power make the right decision! I always knew sponsors would come knocking after a while – I think you have an excellent future ahead of you. However. . ."

"I know, I know," cut in Danny, "*it may not happen, the world is full of disappointments, don't get your hopes up;* my dad has already been through all of that with me!"

."Fine," grinned Alfie. "Adults only ever say this stuff to try and protect kids from having unrealistic expectations."

"Cool," said Danny. "Anyway, Mr Hoult wants to see some footage of me driving. I know we have bits and pieces but do you think you could film me doing more that shows off my range?"

"It would be a pleasure!" smiled Alfie. "Get your

driving gear on and take out the kart you drove on Demo Day. I know it's not world class, but it's good enough to show this Mr Hoult what you can do."

Ten minutes later, Danny, now in full karting gear, was pushing the vehicle out of the kart shed. It was resting on top of a three-wheeled kart trolley. He headed down the slope, then he and Alfie carefully lifted it down trackside. Alfie was carrying the club camcorder, which was a couple of years old but took decent-quality film.

"OK," said Alfie, "do three laps. Don't just go for speed; show your range. Go inside and outside, hug the track like you own it. That should be enough to show Point Power Electronics that you mean business."

As usual, Alfie's encouragements made Danny feel positive and determined.

He climbed into his kart and pulled the seat-belt straps over his karting suit. Alfie handed him his helmet and he slipped it over his head. As Danny hit the TAG – Touch and Go – button, the kart shot forward. Danny gritted his teeth as he approached the first bend of the Sparks Cross track. He was absolutely determined to provide Mr

Hoult with further evidence of his driving abilities. And Alfie was right; it wasn't just about speed, however much Danny loved driving fast.

He imagined he was driving in the Granger Cup Semi-Final. He clung to the middle of the straights and took the corners on the outside, the inside and the centre of the track. He zigzagged, weaving his way through a pack of imaginary drivers. Alfie was at the side of the track, capturing every second of Danny's drive. The three laps went incredibly quickly.

Alfie nodded with satisfaction when Danny pulled in to the start/finish area.

"That was great!" shouted Alfie, spooling back over the footage.

In Alfie's office they downloaded all of the data from the kart's transponder on to Alfie's laptop. This gave detailed data about lap speeds, kart speeds and all other driving information.

"OK," said Alfie, "the second lap was your fastest, but your steering was the tightest on the first, and your braking was the best on the third. I think it's worth sending all of this info as well as the film."

Danny nodded and Alfie started transferring the film from the camera to the laptop.

"Cool!" nodded Danny, eager for Mr Hoult to receive the footage as quickly as possible and show it to the key people so that they could all make a decision – hopefully the right one!

When Alfie was finished, Danny took over the laptop and tapped into his Hotmail account. He typed in Mr Hoult's email address and composed his message.

From: Danny Sharp
To: Frank Hoult
Date: 3rd September
Subject: Driving footage

Dear Mr Hoult

It was excellent to meet you on Monday. I'm sending this from Sparks Cross. I'm attaching a film of me doing three laps on the track here. It wasn't shot under race conditions, but I really hope it shows you what I can do. If you and

Point Power Electronics *do* decide to go ahead with sponsorship, it would be the best thing that's ever happened to me!

Thank you & very best wishes

Danny Sharp

Danny read the message several times and then clicked to attach the footage.

"Go for it!" nodded Alfie.

Danny hit the SEND button.

They waited a few seconds until a sign appeared:

YOUR MESSAGE HAS BEEN SENT.

Alfie took a deep breath. "It's in the laps of the Race Gods now, Danny," he smiled. "Let's hope they look favourably on your karting prowess. If anyone deserves to get a sponsor, it's you."

"Thanks, Alfie."

"It's funny," said Alfie, "the main reason why adults warn kids about getting too excited or expectant about something is because they've suffered their own disappointments and let-downs. I remember how I felt before the crash."

Danny looked at Alfie with fascination. He very rarely mentioned the accident.

"I'd seen my whole future mapped out before me: life as a professional driver, the foreign Grand Prix destinations, the glamorous parties, the champagne flowing and above everything else, victory in a series or more than one."

Danny was hooked on every word.

"All of that expectation, all of those dreams. And then in a few seconds the whole thing was over. I felt my car spin out of control. It smacked against the advertising hoarding and the next thing I knew I was laid out on the grass by the medics and my leg hurt like crazy."

"How did you feel once you found out you couldn't race again?" asked Danny.

"I felt as if my entire future had just been snatched from my grasp and turned to ash. I couldn't believe it."

"It must have been awful."

"It was, for a bit, but then I realized I had two choices. I could either spend the rest of my life being angry at the world and ranting about my lost chances, or I could carry on in the sport by helping others achieve their dreams. Yes, I suppose on one level it was about enjoying success through other people, but it wasn't long before my head was straight again."

"So you're saying that if Point Power Electronics say no, I'll be able to get my head back together and not stay in my bedroom moping for weeks on end?"

"Kind of," grinned Alfie. "I'm saying that life has lots of twists and turns – just like a decent karting track!"

Danny laughed and shook Alfie's hand. "Thanks for filming me today, and thanks for all of the advice you give me," said Danny.

"It's a real pleasure working with someone like you," replied Alfie. "And while I can't gaze into a crystal ball and say you are going to make it up through the ranks, there's no question that you're the best young driver I've ever worked with."

Danny felt a shiver ripple down his spine.

"What are you up to now?" asked Alfie.

A cog clicked into place in Danny's mind.

Home.

Homework.

Supper.

And then the watch press launch with Scot Devlin! He quickly told Alfie about the launch.

"Wow!" exclaimed Alfie. "First a potential sponsor, now Devlin invites you to a posh product launch. This must be Danny Sharp week!"

Danny laughed. "I better head off and get ready," he said, pausing at the doorway of Alfie's office. "Thanks again for being my cameraman!"

"No worries," smiled Alfie. "Have fun tonight; hope you get a freebie watch!"

"A real, genuine, actual product launch!" enthused Carl as the bus neared town.

Danny had managed to get home, do his homework, eat and grab a quick shower before Carl called for him. They were both wearing smart shirts (Danny's blue and white paisley, Carl's light blue button-down), trousers, and black shoes as opposed to their usual trainers.

"Do you think any photographers will be there to take pictures of us?" mused Carl. "If they do, we'll have to be careful about what poses we strike. The world needs to know that you're the future of racing and I'm your manager!"

Danny laughed. "Let's just get in there, see the launch and chat to Devlin. That will get everyone talking about who we are!"

"Who else do you think will be there?" asked Carl. "Any other famous drivers? Or will it just be people from the watch company and a media crowd?"

"I have no idea," answered Danny, who was really looking forward to the event. "Let's just take it as it comes."

"Cool!" nodded Carl.

They got off the bus, walked to the end of the street and turned the corner on to a very long main thoroughfare.

A department store rose up in front of them. Its five storeys towered above the street, its giant glass front doors bearing a six-foot-high COLLINWOOD emblem. Its window displays showed sleek mannequins in a range of outfits, formal and casual, as well as high-end electronic gadgets and top of the range sports gear. About fifteen metres to the left of the main doors, in front of a short flight of stone steps, stood a petite woman with ash-blonde hair. She was wearing a sequinned gold dress and holding a clipboard. At the top of the steps stood two huge men, both with cropped hair and sunglasses, sporting trenchcoats, big boots and suspicious scowls.

"Bouncers," said Danny quietly. "That must be the entrance to the launch."

Carl rubbed his hands together. "Let's do it!" he replied.

They walked up to the woman.

"Er . . . is this where the launch for the Dawn Thread watch is?" asked Danny.

The woman raised an eyebrow suspiciously. "It is," she replied coolly.

"I'm Danny Sharp and this is my friend Carl," explained Danny. "We should be on the list as guests of . . . Scot Devlin."

The woman's other eyebrow joined the first. It looked as if she was about to tell them to clear off, but she quickly scanned the list and her eyes bulged when she came across their names.

"Right," she said, her eyebrows instantly lowering, her tone of voice suddenly friendly.

"Go on in and enjoy the launch," she smiled.

Carl and Danny didn't smile back but proceeded up the steps.

The bouncers nodded at them and one pulled open the door.

They stepped forward and found themselves in a wide corridor with bright purple walls. A large sign stated: *Dawn Thread Watch Launch This Way*, accompanied by an arrow. They followed the arrow round a corner and reached some double doors that were fixed open. A tall woman dressed all in black handed them each a glossy brochure about the watch and a waiter in a bow tie passed by with a tray of tall fluted glasses filled either with champagne or orange juice. Danny and Carl each took an orange juice and entered the launch room.

This was big and rectangular, with high white walls and three ornate chandeliers hanging from the ceiling. A stage had been set up at the far side and this was adorned with huge photos and bits of text about the watch, interspersed with photos of Scot Devlin in

58

different poses at different locations – a beach, a swimming pool, a castle – wearing different versions of the Dawn Thread. There were already about fifty people milling around the room. Danny and Carl studied them, hoping to get a glimpse of someone famous from the racing world, but they were unfamiliar men and women in suits, just chatting and sipping from their glasses. As it neared eight o'clock, more and more people started streaming into the room, and soon the place was packed. The chink of glasses and chatter of voices rose into the air.

Danny and Carl weaved their way through the crowds until they had an excellent position, just a couple of rows back from the stage.

Suddenly the lights in the room were dimmed and a spotlight bathed the stage in a pool of bright whiteness. "Ladies and gentleman," purred a deep dramatic voice, "welcome to Collinwood – one of the world's most prestigious department stores. Here's your host for this evening's launch, CEO of Saramas Leisure, Mr Phillipe Denois!"

To polite applause, a man with long, wavy silver hair

59

and a glittering smile bounded on to the stage. Speaking with a slight French accent, he addressed the audience.

"It's wonderful to see you all here tonight," he smiled charmingly, "but before I introduce you to our special guest, I'd like to show you a short film, highlighting the dramatic innovation we believe we've created in the Dawn Thread, not to mention the elegance and style you've come to expect from our products."

What followed was a five-minute-long, beautifully shot film, showing more footage of Devlin wearing the watch, in helicopters, on frozen mountainsides, at the top of skyscrapers. Accompanying these pictures were flashes of technical info about the watch's "spellbinding" new functions.

"My watch can do most of those things and it only cost me ten pounds," whispered Carl, forcing Danny to suppress a laugh.

The audience responded with applause when the film finished, then Mr Denois showed some huge slides of very close-up images of the watches, with different coloured straps and slightly differing capabilities. Danny was beginning to get bored when the announcement he'd been waiting for arrived.

"And now it is time to introduce the face of the Dawn Thread!" declared Mr Denois. "I give you the Formula One legend, Mr Scot Devlin!"

Blazing music shot out of speakers and bright multicoloured lights pummelled the stage as Devlin walked out, wearing faded designer jeans, a royal blue T-shirt and a Dawn Thread watch, which he held up for the audience to see. The crowd cheered and screamed, no one louder than Danny and Carl. Flashbulbs popped and camera shutters clicked.

"It's great to see you all," beamed Devlin, the audience suddenly quiet. "And I have to say that I genuinely LOVE this product!"

There was laughter from the crowd.

"It's light, it's comfortable and its functions are unbelievably quick and simple. For someone who lives life in the fast lane, the Dawn Thread makes sure I'm never left behind."

There were more shrieks and thunderous applause.

Mr Denois leapt back on to the stage to hug Devlin

and then the Formula One driver leant down and signed some autographs for people in the front row of the audience. Devlin's eyes then seemed to rest on Danny's for a second; was that a nod of recognition? But before Danny could be sure, Devlin gave a final wave to the adoring crowd and was ushered off backstage by a very wiry man wearing a sleek black suit, impossibly narrow gold-framed glasses and a radio earpiece.

Then Mr Denois began taking questions about the watch.

"When this is over we'll hang about near the side of the stage to wait for Devlin," whispered Danny.

Carl gave him a thumbs up.

The Q & A session lasted fifteen minutes. People were then invited to examine different models of the Dawn Thread, which were displayed around the room. Danny spotted several people pulling out credit cards and buying watches on the spot.

But Danny and Carl weren't interested in the watches. As the people began to file out of the room, their excitement levels rose. The few others who stayed were looking at watch brochures and quaffing further glasses of free champagne. The boys sidled over to the side of the stage and peered behind a black curtain. Two tech guys were dismantling the stage while a further two were working on the lights.

"Are you sure we're meant to meet him here?" asked Carl.

"He didn't say," replied Danny, craning his neck to look further backstage and hoping to get a glimpse of Devlin.

Fifteen minutes later and the stage was almost fully dismantled.

"Where is he?" demanded Carl.

"He's probably on the phone to Malloy – his manufacturers – or being interviewed by TV people – something like that," Danny reassured him.

When there was only a handful of people left in the room, the tall woman dressed in black, came up to them with a quizzical look on her face.

"Are you two OK?" she enquired.

"Yeah, we're fine," nodded Danny.

"Actually," chipped in Carl, "we're waiting for Scot Devlin. We're on his guest list and he said he'd hang out with us after the launch."

"Oh dear," she said kindly, "Scot left straight after his appearance. He has another engagement tonight."

Danny felt as if a spike of ice had just been shoved down his throat and he could see from Carl's expression that his best mate felt exactly the same.

"Of c . . . course," said Danny hurriedly, feeling his cheeks redden, "we knew that. He must have meant we'll see him after his next engagement."

The woman pulled a face. "You won't get there unless you can charter a helicopter," she replied. "The next event is in Paris. He's probably halfway over the English Channel by now."

"Right," nodded Carl, trying to cover up his intense disappointment. "We'll . . . er . . . we'll head off then."

"Sorry, guys," she said softly. "Maybe you'll see him another time, yeah?"

But neither of them replied.

They were too choked up.

The only thing they wanted to do was to get as far away from the launch as humanly possible.

"So how did it go?" asked Mum the next morning. She'd been in bed by the time Danny had got home from the launch, while Dad was crashed out on the sofa in front of the TV, so Danny hadn't had a chance to tell either of them anything about his evening and he certainly wasn't going to divulge the truth; it was far too humiliating and he really didn't want their sympathy.

"It was . . . OK," replied Danny, trying to look casual and popping a couple of pieces of bread into the toaster.

Katie was sitting at the table, spooning cornflakes into her mouth.

"Just OK?" frowned Mum.

"Yeah, Devlin had to go to another event straight after the watch thing."

"So you didn't get to spend much time with him?"

"Yeah, it was . . . pretty limited."

"Were you very disappointed?"

"Nah," replied Danny as breezily as he could, "it was cool. There'll be plenty more chances to see him in the future."

Danny knew that Mum sensed all wasn't right, but she didn't push it.

"When will you become a Formula One driver?" asked Katie.

"Not for a while yet," replied Danny, grabbing the toast as it popped up and spreading the slices with margarine. He sat down at the table with Katie. "And I might not make it. It's a long way off and I'll need someone like Mr Hoult to help me out in paying for all of the gear. It gets really expensive when you're older."

"I've got five pounds in my piggy bank," she said.

"You can have it and you don't even need to pay me back."

Danny put his arms round her shoulders. "That's really kind of you," he smiled, "but you keep it. I'll find the money somehow."

Katie's mind quickly changed tracks. "Do women get to be Formula One drivers?" she asked, taking another mouthful of cornflakes.

"At the minute, no," replied Danny.

"That is SO unfair!" protested Katie.

"Women do race in other events," said Danny, "like NASCAR in America, and there's motorcycling too."

"But I want to race in Formula One!" insisted Katie, hitting the table with the palm of her hand.

"It's just one of those things, Katie," said Mum, "some areas of sport are still only open to men. Things are changing, though, and by the time you grow up, there might well be some female F1 drivers."

"There better be!" exclaimed Katie.

As Danny walked to school he went over last night's events in his head for the thousandth time. Why had

Scot Devlin bothered to ask him and Carl to the launch if he wasn't going to spend any time with them? If he'd found out he'd have to shoot off *after* he'd invited them, he could have easily phoned back and told Danny not to show. What was he playing at?

Danny tried hard to put a positive spin on things. Maybe it was a last-minute thing? Maybe he was whisked away by his publicity people? But then he could still have come out and told Danny and Carl he had to go. Danny sighed; unfortunately, however he looked at it, Devlin had badly let him down.

Carl was also in a glum mood when Danny caught up with him.

"What a downer!" said Carl, shaking his head in despair. "I really thought we'd get to spend some time with him; I felt like a right idiot."

"Me too," replied Danny. "There was absolutely no point in us going!"

They were both very down for the rest of the morning, but as the lunch break drew nearer, Carl began to brighten up and he lifted Danny's mood by telling him about all of the flash houses they'd buy round the world when Danny started winning Grand Prix. Jamaica and Spain were first on Carl's list.

"The third should be Italy," suggested Danny.

"Nice one!" grinned Carl. "Pizza whenever we want!"

After lunch Danny and Carl had PE with Mr Neale. To their dismay, Tony Butler's class showed up too, because their PE teacher was off sick.

Danny knew there was going to be trouble the minute he set eyes on Tony, striding into the gym as if it were his personal kingdom. Tony gave him a nasty sneer and whispered something to his best mate, Kev, who laughed.

Mr Neale announced they'd be playing basketball, two 7 v 7 games – each game in a different half of the gym. Danny loved basketball but his last competitive experience had involved him and Carl playing a 2 v 2 game against Tony and Kev on one of the courts in the park. The idea had been that the losers pay the winners twenty pounds. The match had ended in a draw, with no money being owed, but Tony – one of the world's foremost cheats – had disputed Danny's last basket, and the match had ended acrimoniously.

Mr Neale selected four sides of seven players and as luck would have it, Danny and Carl were placed on the same team, while Tony and Kev were put on the opposing team.

"Not again," groaned Danny.

"We'll play for twenty minutes and then take a break," announced Mr Neale.

The twenty minutes were closely fought, with both Danny and Tony netting a couple of baskets for their respective sides. The score was 12-12 when Mr Neale blew for the break. After everyone had taken a drink, Mr Neale said they'd play another twenty.

Ten minutes in, things started turning nasty.

Mr Neale was off refereeing the other game; his eyes were well off Danny's match.

Carl went on an excellent run that saw him swerve and shimmy round three opposition players. He feigned a pass back into defence and bounce passed to Danny, who was positioned just outside the arc. Danny raised his arm to shoot, but suddenly felt a sharp pain in his back. He nearly went down, but staggered a few steps forward and just managed to remain standing.

He looked round and saw Tony Butler a few steps away, looking as innocent as an angel.

"That was bang out of order!" shouted Carl, striding across to Tony and grabbing the ball from him. "What the hell are you doing? You just shoved Danny in the back; you didn't even *try* and get the ball!"

"If he can't take a bit of physical play, he shouldn't be on the court, should he?" snarled Tony.

"That wasn't physical play; that was a foul!" insisted Greg Jensen, another player on Danny and Carl's team.

"Yeah!" nodded Carl emphatically, handing the ball to Danny. "Are you OK, mate?"

Danny nodded but his back felt like it had just been pounded by a hammer. He flashed a filthy glare at Tony and walked to the foul line. After composing himself, he threw his first shot. It missed the basket. But his second dipped through the air, smacked on to the backboard and dropped through the net.

"Yes!!" shouted Danny, clenching his fist in Tony's direction.

Things calmed down in the next play, but soon Tony struck again. A long pass from Greg reached Carl, who threw an overhead pass in Danny's direction. Danny grabbed the ball and headed down court. He'd only gone several paces when Tony shoulder-barged him, hard. Danny was knocked sideways and went crashing to the ground, the ball slipping out of his hands.

The next second, pandemonium broke out on the court. The players from Danny's team started yelling at Tony's team and the two sets of players started squaring up to each other. Danny and Tony were face to face, screaming abuse at each other and shoving each other in the chest.

"WHAT ON EARTH IS GOING ON?" roared an incandescent Mr Neale, running over from the other game; he hurried straight to the centre of the stand-off. One look from him forced the warring players to separate.

"I turn my back for a few minutes and you're at each other like packs of wolves!" he shouted, his eyes alight with fury. "You're not kids – you're teenagers; you should be able to play for a short time unattended. How did this come about?"

The players fell silent.

"Come on, who started it?"

Nothing.

"OK, boys," he said, "you're incredibly lucky today because I should really give the whole lot of you detentions. But I'm not going to because there'll be some amongst you who were less involved than others and I don't believe in collective punishment. But I am very angry with those of you who lost control. I will NOT tolerate any physical violence in my gym; do you get that?"

"Yes, sir," mumbled the players.

"You better be sure," said Mr Neale, "because the next time I see any of you placing even the tiniest finger out of line, you'll be in serious trouble. Now get changed and go!"

The only sounds in the changing room were mutterings from both sides, but as Mr Neale was waiting outside the door, it stayed like this. A raised voice would have brought the full wrath of the PE teacher, and no one could face such a prospect.

"You better watch it!" hissed Tony Butler at Danny and Carl as he and Kev made their way to the door.

"Yeah, yeah!" Danny hissed back. "I am SO terrified!"

"You should be!" scowled Tony. He and Kev exchanged a look and then sidled out of the room.

Danny groaned to himself. Why was Tony Butler allowed to exist in the same time/space dimension as him? Why couldn't he just be powered to some universe billions of miles away and deposited there without a spaceship for the journey back?

"I want you to take a look at this," said Alfie, putting a DVD player into the player. The picture came to life, showing a line of gleaming Formula One cars.

"What's this?" asked Danny.

"It's about acceleration," replied Alfie.

It was four thirty-five p.m. Danny had come straight to Sparks Cross after school, still wound up about the basketball incident with Tony Butler.

"I know some people think the straights are the easiest part of racing," said Alfie, "but that's a myth. Take Sebastian Vettel."

Alfie pressed PLAY and the screen was filled with a shot of Vettel coming out of a corner and storming down a straight in the Malaysian Grand Prix. As he reached a bend, Alfie froze the shot.

"Did you see what he did, Danny? He was already accelerating as he came off the last bend. That's a difficult move to pull off because if you get it wrong, your vehicle will be all over the place. Vettel hit max speed about a third of the way into the straight and then started his brake going into the next bend. That is awesome driving!"

"I try and do that," replied Danny.

"I know you do," nodded Alfie. "But if you're going to improve, you need to study the best."

Alfie pressed PLAY again and there followed a montage of top drivers, both past and present, accelerating down straights: Alonso, Piquet, Coulthard, Barrichello, Button, Hamilton, they were all there. Danny's eyes were fixed on the cars and the tiny details: where exactly on the track they were when they accelerated, what was their position in relation to the other drivers, when did they brake? Danny could quite happily watch this sort of footage for hours on end, but after twenty minutes of these highlights, Alfie pressed STOP.

"Alfie," said Danny, "if Mr Hoult does agree to sponsor me, do you think Point Power Electronics will buy me a new kart?"

"That could be in their package, yes," responded Alfie.

"If I race one of the club karts on Sunday, how much lower will my chances be of making the Granger Cup Final?"

"Don't look at it that way," sighed Alfie. "First of all, some of the club karts aren't bad at all – you know that. And secondly, as I've told you countless times before, the kart is only one part of the equation. The driver is absolutely crucial; a bad driver in a good kart will never win anything."

"What about Tony Butler and his flash new kart?" muttered Danny.

"Tony Butler is a royal pain in the backside, Danny, but he hasn't won here yet. I wouldn't focus on him. The person you need to focus on is yourself. I'm not saying you won't get sponsored, I'm just pointing out that getting a new kart by Sunday is probably a massive long shot. So I suggest you head over to the shed and select your vehicle for the semis. Once you've done that, you can really start focusing on the race."

Alfie chucked him the spare set of club keys.

A minute later, Danny was sliding the shed doors open. He flicked on the light and walked along the row of karts, waiting like battle-ready soldiers, silent and still. He passed the one he'd driven in the demo race on Sunday, number six, and stopped by one with yellow spirals on its side bars: number seventeen. He'd wanted that one for the demo but someone else had booked it out before him. He'd driven it a few times before. If pushed it could just about touch seventy mph; not as fluently as his own kart had been able to do, but to a reasonable standard. Danny had everything crossed that Power Point Electronics would come through in time and he'd have a new kart, but if it did have to be a club kart, this was the one.

He wheeled it away from the others and took a good look at its axles and chassis. They'd seen better days but were in an OK condition. The tyres were in a decent enough state and the metal work in general was acceptable. The steering wheel needed a bit of work. Danny ran his finger down the side bars and thought about the last few days. They'd been totally mad: the Scot Devlin phone call and the disappointment of the watch launch; starting school again; the tension and aggro with Tony Butler; and most importantly the Point Power Electronics situation. He didn't know how much longer he could bear to wait before Mr Hoult got back to him.

Danny reached up to a shelf, pulled down a couple of screwdrivers and started making the necessary adjustments to the wheel. Half an hour later, he was satisfied with his handiwork, so he pushed the kart back to its place and returned to the clubhouse.

"Well, have you chosen?" asked Alfie.

"Yeah," replied Danny. "Seventeen. I made some tweaks on the steering wheel."

"Good work," nodded Alfie. "I'll also give it a look over tonight. Are you going home now?"

Danny nodded.

"Don't forget that DVD I showed you earlier," Alfie

reminded him. "Use the info to improve your driving on Sunday."

"Will do," said Danny.

As he walked up the track back to the main road and the bus stop, his mind was filled with the image of Vettel coming off the corner and accelerating on the straight. If he could drive a tenth as well as Vettel, he'd be overjoyed.

"Have Angie Kelly or Mr Hoult phoned yet?" asked Danny as soon as he walked in the front door.

Mum shook her head. "Don't worry, Danny," she said softly, "Mr Hoult said Friday and I'm sure he'll stick to it; that's only one more night to wait."

After supper Danny was mooching about in his bedroom, unsure what to do with himself, when his mobile rang.

UNKNOWN CALLER.

He took the call.

"Danny, it's Scot Devlin."

Danny said nothing.

"I am SO sorry about last night," said Devlin, "it was a complete mess. My agent had double-booked me so I had to go straight from the watch launch to some charity dinner in France. My agent forbade me from coming over and grabbing a couple of minutes with you and Carl because other people would have crowded us and the whole thing would have held me back."

"I understand," said Danny, who didn't really understand. Surely Devlin could have popped over to say hi, whatever his agent said. Devlin was the star, not the agent. Devlin could have called the shots. Was he just using his agent as an excuse because he couldn't be bothered coming out to speak to Danny and Carl? But then again, Devlin *had* phoned to apologize. Danny's brain ached, thinking about it all.

"I know it must have looked very bad," added Devlin, "but it was out of my hands. Sometimes I spend more time on the showbiz circuit than actually driving my car. It gets ridiculous. Anyway, apart from me letting you down so rudely, how's it going?"

"It's OK," said Danny, trying to sound upbeat. "I'm waiting to hear from that potential sponsor."

"That's great!" enthused Devlin. "If it wasn't for all of the rules governing F1 I'd sponsor you myself!"

"Seriously?" gasped Danny.

"Of course! I've told you – I was just like you when I was your age. My head was totally crammed with F1 dreams. I lived every race I watched on TV."

"That's like me," agreed Danny. "Sometimes I think I take it *too* seriously."

"Nah!" laughed Devlin. "I'm sure you're fine. And anyway, if you look at anyone who has ever made it in their sport, they've committed themselves to it with pretty much everything. If you don't care deeply enough about it you're never going to make it."

"Good point," replied Danny.

"Anyway, I just wanted to let you know that we WILL meet up soon, without me disappearing, OK?"

"Sounds good," answered Danny.

"OK, well, good luck with the sponsor – let me know what happens next time we talk."

"Cool," replied Danny.

Then Devlin was gone.

Danny shook his head and let out a long breath. He was struck by very mixed feelings. On the one hand he was thrilled Devlin had taken the time to call him again, but on the other hand, with a schedule as busy as his, how would Devlin ever be able to fit Danny in? Maybe he just had to take Devlin with a large pinch of salt and not get his hopes up too high.

There – that would please Dad! Danny thought.

"I've told you a million times Danny; the second Angie or Mr Hoult call me, I'll call you. You've got to trust me!"

"I do," sighed Danny, "but the suspense is killing me."

It was Friday morning break and the fifth call Danny had made to his father in the last few hours.

"I know," replied Dad, "but there's nothing we can do except wait."

"Yeah," sighed Danny, "I guess you're right."

"What's your next lesson?" asked Dad, trying to change the subject.

"Music."

"Good," said Dad, "get stuck into it and get your mind off Point Power Electronics. You like music."

"I'll try," replied Danny, but he was in no mood for school or lessons when something so potentially life-changing was hanging over him.

There were still five minutes to go before music when Danny's mobile rang.

"Hi, Danny, it's Alfie. I've had some crucial thoughts about Sunday's race and I want to go over them with you. Could you come here straight after school? The thing is, I can only stay at the club till five thirty tonight because I have a meeting in town at six thirty. What do you think?"

"I'll be there," replied Danny.

Extra advice from Alfie could mean the difference between failure and success.

In the lunch hour Danny made his way to the gym.

Mr Neale nodded at him as he entered and ticked him off the list of people who'd booked a session. That was very Mr Neale – everything was meticulously done by the rules and regulations.

Danny did some warm-up stretches and then made for the exercise bikes. There were a couple of older guys pumping iron. Danny vaguely knew them: Chas and Jem – they were martial arts freaks.

Danny did fifteen minutes on the bike and then fifty sit-ups followed by fifty press-ups before heading to the weights. He selected a couple of dumbbells and started doing some lifts. They were too light so he went up a five kilograms. This was better and he went through a routine of front and side lifts.

Chas and Jem finished up, nodded to Danny and Mr Neale, and then headed off. But as they went through the door, the unpleasant smirking figure of Tony Butler sauntered in.

Danny tried to contain his frustration. Why was Tony everywhere he went?

"All right, sir," nodded Tony to Mr Neale in a manner he thought was cool. Mr Neale clearly didn't think so because he scowled back. But he still ticked him off the list.

Tony went over to the treadmill and started jogging. Danny completely ignored him, reasoning that if he pretended Tony didn't exist then maybe his wish would come true. About five minutes later Mr Neale addressed them both.

"I'm just off to get something from next door; I'll be two minutes max. Can I trust you two to be alone after that disgraceful incident on the basketball court?"

They both nodded.

After the teacher had left, Danny stopped his lifts, replaced the weights and wiped the sweat off his forehead with a towel. He was about to head off towards the showers when Tony called at him from the other side of the room.

"I reckon you'll bottle it before Sunday and pull out of the semis," he sneered.

Ignore him, a voice in Danny's head pleaded, but it was overruled.

"I'll be there!" replied Danny defiantly. "And I'll make it through – unlike you!"

"You reckon?" laughed Tony sarcastically.

"Having a flash kart doesn't make you Jenson Button!" snarled Danny.

"Well, it's better than having *no* kart!" grinned Tony.

Danny felt rage bubbling ferociously inside him and knew that if he didn't walk away now, he couldn't trust himself not to launch himself at Tony. He'd never thrown a first punch, but Tony was pushing him that way. Smarting with fury, Danny turned his back again and started walking away.

But before he'd gone four steps, something big and heavy whistled through the air and went smashing into his left shoulder. Danny yelped in pain, turning quickly to see that Tony had thrown a medicine ball at him.

White-hot sparks of pain shot through Danny's shoulder.

In a couple of seconds he was back on the other side of the room, pushing Tony in the chest. Tony staggered a couple of steps backwards but then hit out with his left fist, catching Danny on the same shoulder.

Danny shouted in agony, swung round and landed a ferocious kick that smashed straight into the centre of Tony's stomach. Tony was thrown to the floor.

"HOW DARE YOU!" bawled Mr Neale, striding into the room. His face was seething with rage, his eyes wide with shock and fury.

In a remarkable slice of play-acting worthy of winning a major dramatic award, Tony burst out crying. "He . . . he . . . attacked me s . . . s . . . sir! It was unprovoked!"

Danny was almost rendered speechless by the enormity of this lie. "That's rubbish, sir. He threw the medicine ball at me first."

Danny's eyes swept round the room, but to his horror, the medicine ball had rolled back towards the rack where it was stored.

Tony writhed about on the floor, groaning in agony.

Mr Neale's eyes flashed between the two of them.

"Please, sir!" urged Danny. "He's lying. I was doing my own thing and he went for me. I was acting in self-defence. I promise you!"

But Mr Neale was shaking his head. "I'm sorry, Danny, but when I came in all I saw was you launching a flying kick at Tony and because of that, I'm placing you in a no-notice detention tonight. I'll be contacting your parents immediately to explain that you're being punished like this because of the severity of your behaviour."

"No, sir, please!" begged Danny.

He had to be out of here the second lessons finished and head straight to Sparks Cross – that's what Alfie had said.

Tony was now thrashing around on the floor issuing pathetic cries of dreadful pain; it was like watching the biggest showman in football trying to convince a referee he deserved a penalty when replays of the incident showed that the only thing he'd come into contact with was air.

"Sir!" tried Danny again. "It was Tony who started it, but if you want to believe him, that's for you to decide. But *please* give me the detention tomorrow, not today. I have to leave school straight away. There's somewhere I have to be."

He thought of the phone call with Alfie about Alfie's crucial pre-race advice. Five thirty p.m. was Alfie's cut-off time and there was no way Danny would ever make it there before six now, because of his detention.

"I'm afraid that's your lookout, Danny. You should have thought of that before you attacked Tony."

Tony slowly got to his feet, wheezing, coughing and spluttering.

Danny's shoulder was killing. The injustice of this whole situation was mind-boggling. He was getting into trouble for a scene that had been dreamed up and started by Tony.

"Tony, I want you to go straight to medical," ordered Mr Neale. "Danny, like I said, I'll be phoning your parents. You're to show up in room thirty-one straight after school; failure to do so will lead to even greater trouble."

Tony shuffled off in his best impression of a severely wounded Vietnam veteran.

"Get changed and go," Mr Neale ordered Danny. "And consider yourself lucky. You know the school's ethos on physical violence. You're lucky to get away with a single detention. I'm being lenient with you because as far as I know you've never been in trouble for this sort of thing before."

After Danny had taken a quick shower and got

changed, he walked to the side of the science block and dialled Sparks Cross. The phone rang and rang but there was no answer. Danny was about to try Alfie's mobile when his own mobile went dead. In all of the worry over Mr Hoult's decision he'd forgotten to charge it!

He cursed himself for being so stupid and raced to the computer rooms to see if Carl was around. He wasn't. Danny checked his watch quickly. If he sprinted to the school office and convinced them to let him use one of their phones, he'd be able to leave a message on Alfie's mobile and get to his next class on time.

He hared down the corridor, burst through some double doors and round a couple of corners until he skidded to a halt outside the school office. The school's main administrator, Mrs Clarke, was OK; Danny's mum vaguely knew her from when they'd been young. She was bound to let him use her phone.

But to his horror, he saw Mrs Clarke and her assistant, Miss Ash, having a very in-depth conversation with a female police officer. Danny groaned. Typical! The one time he really needed the office, its staff were involved in some heavy duty issue with the forces of law and order.

He could barge in there and say he had his own emergency that outweighed whatever it was they were discussing. After all, they weren't using the phones.

He agonized over what to do for a few seconds and then made an approach towards the door. But Mrs Clarke spotted him out of the corner of her eye and gave him the sort of look that says *Stay well away from here!*

Danny grimaced and backed against the wall, willing the policewoman to hurry up and finish her business, whatever it was, but he was still waiting when the three-minute-warning buzzer went – signalling that the afternoon's lessons were about to start. Danny felt like screaming with frustration, but he was already in enough trouble with Mr Neale and didn't fancy having detention on consecutive days.

This was infuriating! He couldn't contact Alfie and he couldn't get out of detention. It was as if the world was against him while Tony Butler got nothing but goodwill and approval.

Detention was dreadful and seemed to drag on for ever, but at least Danny managed to secretly charge his phone. There were eight kids and they had to sit in absolute silence while finishing their homework for an hour and a half.

As soon as they were let out, Danny checked his voicemail. There was one from Alfie:

"Hi, Danny. My six-thirty meeting has been called off so I'll be here for ages. If you can still make it, do so!"

Yesss!

Just after six fifteen p.m., Danny was running down the path leading to Sparks Cross.

"What have you got for me?" he panted, bursting into Alfie's office.

"A mate of mine did some technical work on the track at Hardy Bridge a while back," grinned Alfie, "and he sent me this."

He held up a DVD.

"He took some in-depth visuals of the track. It's seriously detailed, far better than anything we've looked at on the Internet. I only thought about it last night and he had it couriered over to me this afternoon."

"Alfie – you're amazing!" exclaimed Danny. Hardy Bridge was the track where the Granger Cup Semi-Final was going to be held. Having this kind of knowledge would be a massive help on race day.

"I aim to please!" laughed Alfie. "Shall we check it out?"

"Definitely!" nodded Danny.

Alfie loaded the disk into his computer and a huge 3D image of the track at Hardy Bridge filled the TV screen.

"OK," began Alfie, "as you can see, the track has three straights and seven bends. Let's start with the most difficult part of the course."

"Cool," nodded Danny, whose face was almost pressed against the screen.

Alfie flicked a few more keys and a bird's eye view of Bend 7 appeared.

"Bend 7 is a long triple apex, one of the longest corners you'll ever face as a junior in this sport," explained Alfie. "It has very high G-levels and lots of drivers come unstuck there. You'll have to expertly judge your speed going in and out."

"Got it," mouthed Danny.

Alfie swept over the course and froze the image again.

"The third straight is by far the longest and realistically this provides your best overtaking opportunity. Remember Vettel! The track in general is pretty fast and free-flowing, but there are sections which are bumpy, mainly around Bends 3 and 4 – you'll have to watch your braking very carefully in this area."

"OK," replied Danny, who was drinking everything in with deep concentration etched on his face.

"And as you can see, barriers line the track and aren't set back from it. That means more than ever, you need to concentrate every single second. No daydreaming about future glories, Danny; eyes on the track."

"Absolutely!" nodded Danny.

For the next hour they went over the Hardy Bridge track, section by section, discussing every aspect of the course in minute detail.

Alfie finally put up his hand to indicate it was time to stop. "You should be getting home, Danny, and I should be locking this place up."

"That was brilliant!" said Danny, who'd never studied a track in such detail. Knowing exactly what to expect slightly alleviated his anxiety about driving in a club kart.

"I'm glad you got something out of it. Do you need a lift up to the bus stop?" said Alfie, reaching for his keys.

"Nah, I'm fine, thanks," replied Danny.

He said goodbye and started walking back up the drive. He'd just reached the main road when he spotted his mum driving down towards him in her blue Ford Fiesta. Danny realized that in all of the anger and resentment with Tony and Mr Neale, and the excitement of studying the Hardy Bridge track at such close quarters, he hadn't phoned her to let her know about the detention and the fact he'd be back late. She pulled up beside him and wound down her window.

"I thought you'd be here," she said. "Mr Neale phoned and told me something about you lashing out at another boy – that is so not like you! He also told me you got a detention!"

"He got it all wrong," huffed Danny, "I promise you. The other kid hit me first, so I kicked him."

"Who was he?" asked Mum.

"No one you know," replied Danny. He deliberately withheld the truth because Dad knew Tony's father, Mike Butler, and they didn't exactly see eye-to-eye. "It just happened that Mr Neale missed the first act and saw the second one."

She studied Danny's face for a few seconds. "I believe you," she said, "but you've never had a detention for fighting before and I don't want you getting one again."

"I won't," replied Danny wearily, opening the passenger door and easing down into the seat. He winced as the seat belt brushed against his shoulder. He'd blocked out the pain when he'd been with Alfie but now it hit him. That medicine ball had been seriously heavy.

Danny was quiet at supper, glancing at his watch every few seconds, half-heartedly quizzing Katie about her new teacher and half-listening as she regaled him with a long and convoluted story about a mini-netball match.

After supper, Danny paced the kitchen.

"I can't believe Mr Hoult or Angie hasn't called yet!" he muttered irritably. Katie was desperate to stay up to see if one of them phoned but Mum said no and after a short battle, Katie was dispatched to bed.

"Try and relax," offered Dad, who looked as nervous

as Danny. "Mr Hoult is a very busy man – he won't have forgotten you. He's probably just got a million other things to do as well."

"But it's well past eight!" protested Danny. "Surely he has to finish work at some point?"

"Managing directors of big companies aren't nine to fivers," replied Dad. "They have hundreds of things on the go; just try and be patient for a little longer."

Danny was about to start pacing again when Dad's mobile rang.

It was as if the air had suddenly been sucked out of the room. Danny and his parents froze where they were. But then Dad snapped out of it and pressed to take the call.

Danny had never concentrated so hard on anyone's face. He wanted to pick up Dad's reactions from the tiniest facial-muscle movement. Mum was watching Dad in exactly the same hawk-like way. For at least two minutes Dad's face was completely expressionless. It was agony to watch him and have absolutely no idea what Mr Hoult was saying. But then there was a slight downwards turn of his lips.

Danny instantly knew it was a no.

Disbelief and crushing disappointment coursed through him.

"I see," Dad was saying sombrely. "Yes, I completely understand."

Danny put his face in his hands. How could anyone be so cruel? He and Dad had met Mr Hoult; he'd liked them, he'd given them hope, and now he was dropping them like a lead weight? Danny uncovered his eyes in time to see Dad releasing a long, drawn-out sigh. And then suddenly Mum was striding across the room and taking the phone out of Dad's hand.

"Mr Hoult, it's Julie Sharp here, Danny's mum. I can see from my husband's face that you have decided not to back Danny. I know that you've been totally upfront about everything and that you promised Danny nothing. But, how can I put this . . . driving is Danny's life. It really is. He's a great kid – always keeps up with his schoolwork, doesn't cheek the teachers – at least not very often – and is one of those people that everyone warms to. I wasn't interested in his karting until a few weeks ago. I didn't want to watch him because I was nervous about the safety aspects. But then I went and saw him in the quarter-final of the Granger Cup and it was amazing. It really was. The way he handled that kart, the determination, the burst of speed when it was needed . . . it was almost artistic. His dad and I back him as much as we can but there's no way we'll ever be able to get him all of the gear and entry fees and other things he'll need if he wants to go any higher in the sport. I know I'm his mum, but I genuinely think he's got something. I'm not begging and I'm not expecting you to instantly change your mind on account of me ranting at you, but please! Give him another chance!"

There was silence in the room as Mum listened to Mr Hoult's response to her passionate outburst. Following this, she spoke again.

"Thank you, Mr Hoult. I appreciate your time."

She pressed the end call button on the phone.

"Well?" asked Dad.

She shook her head, walked over to Danny and put her arms round his shoulders. "There are plenty of other companies out there," she said quietly. "You'll find someone to sponsor you. All of the good drivers do."

Danny felt the urge to cry but tears didn't come. A great empty ache pounded in the centre of his chest. All of his dreams about getting a brand new kart in time for Sunday's semi-final had just turned to ashes and drifted out of the window. He'd have to drive the Sparks Cross kart, facing Tony Butler in his flash machine and all of the other semi-finalists in their sleek karts. It wasn't fair! Why had Frank Hoult called him in and raised his hopes, only to reject him? The clips of Danny driving that he and Alfie had emailed to Mr Hoult were good enough to show anyone who knew anything about driving that Danny was talented. Weren't they? Maybe Danny had got too high an opinion of himself? What if he was just Mr Average? That way, new kart or no new kart, he may as well give up on the entire Formula One dream, as he'd never get anywhere near the Grand Prix circuit. Bitterness and dejection frothed inside him.

"Look, mate. . ." began Dad, but Danny barged past him and ran up to his room.

He slammed his door shut and threw himself face down on to the bed, hot tears of rage and disappointment finally rolling down his cheeks. Alfie and Dad had been right all along. *Don't get your hopes up;* that's what they'd said. If only he'd listened to them and not let his mind wander into visions of gleaming motorsport success. Mr Hoult and Point Power Electronics wouldn't be backing him and that was that. How could he have been such an idiot and got so carried away?

There was a gentle knock on his door.

"It's Dad. Can I come in?"

"GO AWAY!" shouted Danny.

Hurt and humiliation swirled around his head for another ten minutes until there was another knock on the door.

Dad again.

"Come on, mate; let's talk about this."

This time Danny couldn't even be bothered to tell his father to leave him alone. It was as if all of the strength had been squeezed out of him.

The door handle turned and Dad slowly entered. He sat on the chair by Danny's desk.

"Come on, Danny," said Dad quietly.

Danny sighed wearily, turned over and sat up on his

bed. He wiped his tears with the back of his sleeve and his eyes met Dad's.

Dad's face was shadowed with concern.

"I know it's terribly upsetting that Mr Hoult didn't come through," began Dad. "I mean, we met him and everything; it seemed so promising. . ."

Danny said nothing.

". . .but Mum's right. Point Power Electronics is just *one* potential sponsor. Remember, I only wrote to *twenty* companies. There are literally thousands more out there. In the morning I'll send out another batch of enquiry letters. I promise you. Except this time I won't send them to twenty companies, I'll send them to a hundred or more; how about that?"

Danny shrugged his shoulders.

"We'll find a sponsor, I know we will."

"I don't think so," snapped Danny. "What happens if we never even get a meeting with someone again?"

"We will," stated Dad.

"If we don't find a sponsor pretty quickly, there's no way I can carry on driving," said Danny quietly. "You know how much the costs increase in the older categories.

Formula Ford, Formula Renault – we're talking tens of thousands and then hundreds of thousands. It's a non-starter unless someone backs me."

"I wish taking on a few more shifts at work could deliver the goods," said Dad, regretfully.

Danny scratched the side of his face and said nothing. Dad worked hard enough already – Danny didn't expect him to kill himself.

"Look, mate, you've got the Granger Cup Semi-Final on Sunday and I don't want you moping around before it, thinking negatively about everything and doing your chances down."

"But I'll be driving a club kart, Dad – they're rubbish – we both know they are."

"They might not be top spec, but they're not rubbish," said Dad firmly. "If you're on your game, there's no reason you can't make it to the final driving one of them."

Danny frowned in disagreement.

"I know you feel defeated, but I suggest you try and put it out of your mind and get some sleep."

Put the biggest disappointment of my life out of my

mind? thought Danny. *That's going to be slightly easier said than done!*

Dad stood up, gave Danny a pat on the shoulder and left his room. As soon as he was gone, Mum walked in.

"I'm not a member of the royal family!" protested Danny. "You don't have to queue up to see me!"

He immediately felt bad about saying this. His mum had tried so hard to get Mr Hoult to give him a chance; she'd really battled for him. He'd never heard her speak that way before.

"All I want to say is that your dad, Katie and I all really believe in you and think you have a great future in the sport. Don't let one disappointment cloud your mind."

Danny managed a half smile and his mum left.

He lay on his bed for ages staring into space, letting the bad news wash over him. However much he wished that Mr Hoult's decision had been different, it hadn't been. Danny had to face the stark fact that the search for a sponsor had been smashed back to stage one.

For the first few moments after waking up on Saturday, Danny was blissfully unaware of the events from the previous night, but then it all hit him like a blow to the centre of his stomach.

Mr Hoult's rejection hurt just as badly today as it had yesterday. Danny knew he'd have to do as Dad said and get over it, and hope that another sponsor would come on board, but Danny wasn't sure he could do that. He grabbed some toast and a cup of tea from the kitchen and headed outside. He'd go for a run to try and clear his head.

Ten minutes later, Danny climbed over a stile and landed in a large field. He put some earbuds in his ears, flicked on the music player on his mobile and started running. Soon his arms were pumping the air, his heart was thudding and sweat was dripping down his face. But while running normally made him feel good, Danny felt weighed down by his current situation. Thirty minutes in and he couldn't shake the waves of despair washing over him.

Everything related to karting seemed bleak. The rejection from Mr Hoult was a body blow however Danny looked at it. And he couldn't stop returning to the fact that he'd be driving a club kart tomorrow. He had tried to reason with himself but it was no good. While Tony Butler would be speeding in his shiny new kart, Danny would be pushing an old model as hard as its aged parts could go.

He knew what Dad and Alfie always told him:

It's not the kart, it's the driver.

A bad workman blames his tools.

But these clichés were just like the legendary one issued by PE teachers the world over:

It's not the winning; it's the taking part that counts.

Could you imagine someone saying to any Formula One driver: *So you came last in that Grand Prix, no need to worry – at least you took part!*

Danny laughed bitterly to himself, slumped down on to the ground and rested his back against the base of a giant oak tree. His shoulder still ached. The sky was a cloudless blue and the smell of the freshly cut grass filled his nostrils.

As Danny pictured in his mind the kart he'd selected to drive, he realized that he was setting himself up to fail – no matter what Alfie or anyone else said. It wouldn't be a fair fight against Tony and the other finalists. And that sucked! Danny put his head in his hands. He'd never felt at such a low ebb. It had been one bad thing heaped upon another. His normal ability to cheer himself up wasn't working and it was a horrible feeling. Danny closed his eyes and made a decision.

I'm not going to be humiliated and have Tony Butler gloating in my face for the next year. With his flash kart he'll probably make the Granger Cup Final and I'll be left for dust.

I'm pulling out of the race.

Even though the morning was warm, Danny shivered.

He stood up, turned round and started to jog home, his spirits heavier by the step at the prospect of breaking the news.

"You're making a terrible mistake!" cried Dad.

They were standing in the kitchen facing each other a metre apart. Mum was upstairs washing Katie's hair, out of earshot.

"I've made up my mind," said Danny firmly. "I'm not racing so there's no point in talking about it."

"Of course there is!" exclaimed Dad. "This is the biggest race of your life! How do you hope to ever get sponsorship if you don't take a chance like this?"

"You've seen the club karts, Dad. They're not a patch on what the others are like!"

"But your skills as a driver outweigh the disadvantages of the kart!" cried Dad. "You could win that race driving a far worse vehicle."

"That's rubbish and you know it!" replied Danny.

"Please, Danny! You can't pull out! Think of all the hard work you've put in to get to this point!"

"But that was in my own kart, Dad! Which is smashed to pieces, if you hadn't noticed!"

"Come on, Danny. It'll look really bad! What will Alfie say?"

"I don't care how it looks!" snapped Danny. "I'm not driving in a race that I know I have no chance of winning or coming in second or third. I'll trail the pack and fail! I'm not driving and that's final!"

"Danny!"

"NO!"

"What's going on in here?" Mum had entered the kitchen and was looking at them with big, concerned eyes.

"Dad will tell you!" snarled Danny, hurrying out, stamping down the hall and leaving the house. He walked with his head down and his hands in his pockets. He had no destination in mind; he just wanted to be away from everyone. He walked past the local shops, over the road and in the direction of the old paint factory. The yard at the back was completely deserted. He sat down on a crumbling brick wall and pulled out his phone and headphones. Turning the volume to loud, he closed his eyes, flicked on a playlist he'd compiled last week and tried to shut the world out.

It was about twenty minutes later when he felt his phone vibrate. He pulled it out.

ALFIE PRICE read the caller display.

Danny really didn't feel like talking to Alfie but he answered it anyway.

"Danny? Your dad just left a message on my mobile. He told me what happened with Mr Hoult and some nonsense about you pulling out of the semi-final."

"It's not nonsense. I'm not driving tomorrow."

"I don't accept your decision."

"What do you mean you don't accept it?" shouted Danny angrily. "It's *my* decision to make!"

"Just hear me out," said Alfie.

"Please, Alfie," said Danny, trying to calm down. "I really don't want to talk about it."

"Well I do!" said Alfie rather fiercely. "I've spent years working with you on building up your driving experience and your ability and I'm not prepared to see that all go up in smoke."

"It's only one race," said Danny, sulkily.

"No it's not!" retorted Alfie. "It's the semi-final of a national competition! You have no idea who'll be there. There might be serious potential sponsors, talent scouts, maybe even someone from one of the leading manufacturers' teams. You can't afford not to be there. What if it's a real bite of the cherry and you're a no show?"

Danny said nothing for a few seconds as he mulled over Alfie's words. He knew Alfie meant well but Danny was in no mood for backtracking.

"Yeah, Alfie, and how bad would it look if I turn up there in a rubbish kart and all of those talent spotters and sponsors see me drive a pathetic race and roll in last! I'll really stick in their minds then, won't I? *Oh yeah, that Danny Sharp kid – the pathetic little loser!*"

"Look, Danny, there's no point in discussing this any more over the phone. I've got to make a phone call and if all goes to plan then I'll pick you up later. I'll be at your house at about one p.m."

"What are you talking about?" demanded Danny.

But Alfie had already cut the call.

Danny considered staying out and not being around when Alfie came over, but his curiosity just about got the better of him and after a long while he returned home. He mumbled an apology to his parents for storming out on them and then lay on his bed moping.

Alfie arrived spot on one p.m. in his ex-army jeep.

"Hi Alfie," called Dad, after opening the front door.

"Hi, Ed. I need to borrow your son for a couple of hours," smiled Alfie.

"I think I can loan him out for that long," replied Dad, "but please bring him back in one piece."

"I guarantee safe return delivery!" laughed Alfie.

"What's going on?" asked Danny warily, coming downstairs and loping outside.

"Just get in and you'll find out," replied Alfie mysteriously.

Danny sighed, nodded goodbye to Dad and then followed Alfie into the jeep.

"Er . . . where are we going?" asked Danny as Alfie drove out of Grassmere Close.

"You'll see shortly," came the reply.

"What's with the secrecy?" said Danny sulkily. "You're not going to change my mind."

"I know I'm not," nodded Alfie.

"So what's the point of this outing?" demanded Danny, starting to get riled by Alfie's lack of details.

"Just hang in there and you'll see," replied Alfie.

Danny shook his head and gazed out at the scenery. In five minutes they had left the paved streets and houses and were speeding along a country lane. They drove cross-country for about fifteen miles, hit an A road for another five miles and then followed a long winding dirt track that passed a dilapidated barn and the entrance to a farm. A small metal gate blocked the track.

"Open the gate," instructed Alfie.

"What are we doing, Alfie?" Danny was hot and irritable. "I don't want to go on some stupid field trip."

Danny had never spoken like that to Alfie before but he was past caring.

"The gate," repeated Alfie, who didn't seem at all bothered by Danny's harsh tone.

Danny sighed heavily, got out and opened the gate. Alfie drove through and Danny closed the gate behind him before climbing back into the passenger seat. They drove round the left curving edge of the field, with a long line of beech trees on their left. Alfie then made a sharp turn and the jeep crossed over a narrow bridge into another large field. This one was overgrown with weeds and reedy grass but you could see stretches of tarmac showing through the gaps.

But it wasn't the surroundings that caught Danny's eye.

It was the car standing about twenty metres away.

Danny gasped in awe.

It was a Ferrari 458 Italia in metallic red. He knew the car well. Its spec was unbelievable: 8 cylinders, a mid-rear mounted engine, a dry weight of 1,380 kg, forged wheels, a racing seat, and a dual-clutch 7-speed Formula

One gearbox with a max speed of 202 kmh. That was what you called a sports car.

Its driver door swung open and out climbed . . . Scot Devlin.

Danny looked from Devlin to Alfie and then back again in amazement.

Alfie grinned and got out of the jeep. On wobbly legs, Danny followed suit. Devlin strode over to meet them. He was wearing faded jeans and a bright blue polo neck with a white baseball cap perched on his head and a thin silver chain round his neck. He shook Alfie's hand.

"The places I end up!" he said with a mock groan, after which he shook Danny's hand.

"I don't get it," mouthed Danny.

"I'll leave you two gents alone," nodded Alfie. "Scot will make sure you get home OK."

Seconds later Alfie's jeep revved up and disappeared from view.

Danny had no idea what the hell was going on. And yes, he'd been this close to Devlin before, but apart from a few minutes here and there, he'd never been alone with him.

"Sorry," said Danny slowly, "but what are we doing in a dead field?"

"Aha!" grinned Devlin. "A dead field is what it looks like now, but that wasn't always the case."

"Is this something to do with farming?" enquired Danny with bewilderment.

"No," replied Devlin, "this place had a former life. It used to be called Print Park Karting Club."

Danny looked around.

The tarmac suddenly made sense.

"Print Park was where *I* got started, Danny. This overrun place was where my dreams were first formed. You're not the only one whose head is full of dreams. For about ten years, this was my second home, maybe even my first home! Every spare second I spent here."

He started walking to the centre of the field with Danny right behind him. Danny still felt angry and despondent but there was no way he was going to pass up an opportunity to spend some more time with Devlin.

"All around us was the track," explained Devlin, pointing to various places. "Five bends and four straights. We're just walking over Bend 2. I nearly had a major crash at this exact spot but managed to swerve out of the way at the last second. Over there, a boy did crash. His name was Kelvin. He broke his left arm."

Danny looked at the weeds and tried to imagine the place with a twisting track.

"That was the start line," went on Devlin, indicating up to the right of the field, "and that was the finish." He pointed down the field and to the left. "I won my first-ever trophy here. I was ten and it felt like I was world champion!"

"Sorry," said Danny, "but I don't see. . ."

Devlin ignored him and continued. "Out on this track I felt like king of the world. It was here that I decided I wanted to pursue driving professionally. My dad died when I was five so I was brought up by my mum. She followed my interest in motorsport and taught herself about racing. She was and still is my biggest fan. She held down two jobs just to keep me in karting gear. I was lucky enough to be spotted at eleven and a sponsor came through. But without my mum's encouragement, I'd never have got anywhere."

Danny listened with interest. He didn't know much about Devlin's past. He tried to imagine how nightmarish it would have been if his own dad had died when he was five. It didn't really bear thinking about.

Devlin started walking to the far side of the field. "The clubhouse was over there," he smiled. "It was a right old dive, but the couple who ran the place, Vera and Dave Bagshott, were absolutely brilliant – very much like Alfie; solid people who really cared about the members."

"Is that why I'm here?" asked Danny. "To see where you got started?"

"Yes, but it's far more than that, Danny. When Alfie told me about your decision to withdraw from tomorrow's race, we thought it would be a good idea to bring you down here."

Danny looked blank.

"Can't you see, Danny? This is where I started and now I'm a professional F1 driver; this patch of overgrown grass, cracked concrete and sprouting weeds got me started. It's now a tip, but even when it was fully functioning it was very basic."

"What are you saying?" asked Danny.

"I'm saying you HAVE to race in the semi-final tomorrow. I'm saying that pulling out would be something you'll regret, possibly for the rest of your life!"

"But the other riders will all have amazing karts!" replied Danny sourly.

"Listen, Danny, I can totally see where you're coming from with regard to driving a club kart instead of a better model – but we can't always drive the vehicle we want. My first kart was a completely battered third-hand affair, but I still drove it with massive pride. You and loads of kids your age today would probably have scoffed at it – called it a heap of junk – but to me it was like one of the Crown Jewels."

Danny rubbed his eyes, trying to take in the surreal nature of the position he found himself in; he was being petitioned by his Formula One hero to race in the Granger Cup Semi-Final. What was he going to do? Thank Devlin for the pep talk and then chuck it back in his face?

"What do you say?" Devlin pressed him.

Danny stamped down some weeds with the sole of his trainer. "I don't want to give up," he mumbled, "but it feels like everything is against me. You said yourself that you got a sponsor when you were eleven. I'm *fourteen* and there isn't a sponsor in sight. It feels like it's all over for me."

"That's rubbish!" exclaimed Devlin. "Loads of drivers get sponsors when they're well into their teens. It's early days – that's not something to fret about. If you carry on driving well, a sponsor will show up; trust me on that."

Danny sighed uncertainly.

"Look," said Devlin, scratching his chin thoughtfully. "Alfie Price is one of the wisest heads in this sport and if he says you have real talent then that's good enough for me. But to make it as a driver you have to be able to deal with setbacks. Remember last year in Monte Carlo when I allowed a couple of drivers to pass me on Bend 7 in the fifth lap? It cost me the race. No one can have a life without the downs as well as the ups. You need to rethink this decision."

Danny chewed his bottom lip. A bird chirruped a call somewhere in the distance.

"Come on, Danny! Why would I traipse all the way out here to my old stomping ground if it wasn't for a very good reason? I came for you because I think your commitment to the sport is first class and I'd hate you to give up now when there's still so much good stuff ahead of you. You have to believe things will turn around. You have to believe in yourself!"

Danny scratched his cheek.

"What do I have to do, mate? Lie down on the track here and beg you?"

Danny couldn't suppress a slight smile; the thought of Scot Devlin prostrating himself and begging was a funny one.

"So come on, Danny, what do you say?"

Danny took a deep breath.

"OK," he sighed, "I'll do it. But if I make an absolute idiot of myself I'm blaming you."

"That's the spirit!" cried Devlin, slapping him on the back. "If it all goes badly, I'll get you T-shirts made proclaiming SCOT DEVLIN RUINED MY RACING CAREER!"

Danny laughed, but then turned serious again. "If I do manage to make it through the semi, though, I don't think a club kart will cut it in the final."

"All right, I accept that and that's something we can look at, but for the time being you need to get ready for the semi-final and I think the first stage of that process involves having a spin in the Ferrari."

"Really?" exclaimed Danny.

"Yeah!" grinned Devlin. "I guarantee it will make everything seem better!"

They headed back down the field towards the gleaming red car.

They got in, pulled on their seat belts and Devlin gunned the engine.

The next five minutes were some of the most glorious of Danny's life. The tarmac covering the field wasn't exactly what you'd call even, but the Ferrari handled it brilliantly. There were bursts of speed, turns and zigzags, screeching tyres and clouds of dust. Devlin looped a final figure of eight and skidded to a halt.

"That was AMAZING!" breathed Danny.

"Glad you enjoyed it," smiled Devlin. "Now all I need to do is get you home."

On the way back to Danny's house, Devlin flicked on the Ferrari's streamlined music system and blasted some r 'n' b out of the speakers. Danny sat back and thought about tomorrow's race. Just because he'd agreed to drive in it didn't mean he rated his chances. Plus, the thought of him not qualifying for the final and Tony Butler succeeding still stuck in his gullet. But having Scot Devlin convince him to race had shown him he'd be stupid to just give up. People really believed in him. The only thing Danny could do now was to try and push all of the negative thoughts and doubts to the back of his mind.

Devlin turned off the music when they pulled into Grassmere Close.

"Why did you do this for me?" asked Danny, when Devlin pulled the Ferrari to a stop outside the Sharps' house.

"I told you: you remind me of myself at your age. If I can put anything back into the sport, I will. Besides, having let you and Carl down at the watch launch, this was the least I could do. Unfortunately I can't be at the race tomorrow, but I'll be willing you on, Danny. You can count on that!"

They shook hands and Danny climbed out.

"Good luck!" nodded Devlin.

Danny patted the roof of the Ferrari; then Devlin spun in an arc and powered his way out of the close.

"Was that a Ferrari 458?" asked Dad, who had been looking out of the window when Danny and Devlin arrived. Now he was out in the street.

"Yeah," nodded Danny.

"And the race?" asked Dad anxiously.

"I'm back in it," replied Danny, his downturned lips moving upwards to form the faintest of smiles.

"So Devlin delivered?" mouthed Dad in wonderment. "Alfie said he'd give him a ring, but I didn't think he'd come through for you; a guy like that has huge pressures on his time."

"Yeah, he came through," nodded Danny, "and he

convinced me. But next time you and Alfie hatch a plan involving an F1 superstar, could you give me a little bit of warning?"

Dad laughed. "Come inside," he said. "We need to start getting ready for tomorrow."

"Wake up, Danny! It's the race today!"

Danny's eyelids opened slowly and the sight of Katie hovering over the end of his bed with a giant piece of paper in her hand greeted him.

"It's your good-luck card," she explained, handing it over.

Not only was it giant; the amount of work she'd put into the card was staggering. The front cover had a huge picture of him racing round a track in a bright purple kart with hundreds of individually drawn spectators cheering him on. Katie, Mum and Dad were drawn far bigger than everyone else and they were holding a banner saying GO DANNY! The inside of the card had another huge scene, this one of Danny holding a giant silver trophy above his head, surrounded by a phalanx of photographers.

"Wow, Katie, it's amazing!" he laughed, pulling her towards him and giving her a hug. "Thank you!"

"Are you coming down for breakfast?" gushed Katie. "Mum said she'll do pancakes!"

"Er . . . not quite yet," replied Danny. "It's only half past seven and I'm going to try and get some more sleep – you know, get in the best shape for the race."

Katie's face dropped for a few seconds but then she was off out of the room, calling down to Mum about how much Danny liked her card.

It was just after nine a.m. when Danny finally rolled out of bed. He had a long soak in the shower, then put on jeans and a black T-shirt and went downstairs. Mum was there to greet him.

"What do you fancy?" she enquired. "Pancakes or cereal?"

"Cereal," replied Danny.

"How are you feeling?" asked Mum.

"Nervous, but not too bad; the real anxiety will kick in later."

"Well, whatever happens, we're all proud of you. If you do make it through to the final, then brilliant! If you don't, then there'll be other finals. You're in it for the long haul, aren't you?"

Danny nodded and pulled a bowl out of the cupboard.

By ten a.m. the nerves were pounding through him. The race was at two thirty p.m. He'd need to leave at about eleven thirty. What was he going to do for the next hour and a half?

Luckily Carl showed up and regaled Danny with non-stop stories about what they would do about the fame and fortune that awaited them in the near future. The Lear jets they'd own, the Hollywood premieres they'd attend, the butlers they'd employ. Danny laughed so hard he wished he had his rib protector on.

"All right, lads," said Dad, coming into the kitchen bang on the dot of eleven thirty a.m. "Let's make a move."

Dad had already packed a picnic and Danny's racing gear into the back of the Fiat Doblo.

"Just remember to try and relax and enjoy it," said Mum, standing beside the Doblo with Katie. "I know how big a deal it is, but it's also just another race and you've won loads of those before."

"Cheers!" replied Danny, as he and Carl took the passenger seats and Dad climbed into the driver's side.

"Katie and I will see you down there a bit later," said Mum as she and Katie waved them off.

"Granger Cup Semi-Final, here we come!" exclaimed Carl as Dad hit the accelerator and they set off. It was great having Carl on the journey. He kept up a constant stream of discussion/commentary/prediction about the other cars on the road. Danny and Dad mostly listened, chucking in the odd comment. They stopped at Sparks Cross to pick up kart seventeen, the one Danny would be driving. Alfie had given Danny the spare keys to the kart shed. Once it was loaded into the back of the Doblo, they were off again.

When they arrived at Hardy Bridge, just after twelve p.m., the place was already a hive of activity. There were vans, estate cars and trailers parked in rows. Adults and children both in karting gear and civvies moved round the vehicles, some pushing karts on trolleys, some chatting to friends, some carrying spanners and wrenches.

Dad pulled into an empty space, and a minute later he and Danny were lifting the kart out of the back of the van. They placed it on the floor and knelt down to take a close look. They spent about twenty minutes checking it over. Everything seemed to be in decent shape and Danny forced himself not to shoot too-envious glances at other karts in the vicinity, but there were quite a few of them and he couldn't help thinking they all looked a million times better than the one he'd be driving.

Just before one p.m. Alfie showed up.

He shook everyone's hands and gave Danny an encouraging wink. The four of them then set up some foldable camping chairs behind the van and Dad brought out a rucksack packed with cheese and pickle sandwiches, crisps, apples and cans of Coke.

"Don't forget that I'm here as a spectator, not as a race official," Alfie reminded Danny, "so if you want advice or an ear to listen, I'm here for you."

"Thanks," replied Danny, massively reassured to have his mentor here and to be able to sit and talk to him, rather than just see him hurrying around the place dealing with everyone else's issues, which was the case on race days at Sparks Cross.

Danny took a couple of bites out of a sandwich and began a conversation with Carl about who would get into the school basketball team this season.

After eating, Danny told the others he was going for a short stroll.

"Shall I come with you?" offered Carl.

"No, it's OK. I just want to get my head together before the race."

"Cool," nodded Carl.

Danny cut through between a huge blue camper van and a yellow lorry and followed the path in the direction of the organizers' hut – a steel affair that looked like a huge shipping container. Wherever he looked people were attending to karts: slotting tyres in place, checking brake fluid levels, tinkering with steering wheels. As well as the Granger Cup Semi-Final there was a host of other races on at Hardy Bridge today and the tension and excitement in the early September sunshine was palpable.

There was a lot of bustle and business inside the organizers' hut. People were checking in for races, discussing tactics and buying stuff from the mini store that set up on practice and race days. Danny picked up a new book about karting and skim-read the first couple of chapters. It was very technical, but he liked that; there was always reams more stuff to learn.

He nodded a greeting to a couple of kids he'd seen before at Sparks Cross and then decided to head back to Carl, Dad and Alfie. He chose to take a different route back, stepping past a large gazebo that was attached to a caravan, in which three karts were getting the once-over by what looked like seven members of the same family.

Danny was halfway back to base when he spied Tony Butler.

There he was, with his dad, Mike, kneeling down beside his glittering kart, wielding a screwdriver in his hand as if he were a techie at the world's most sophisticated race meeting.

Tony looked up and clocked Danny. He muttered something to his father, stood up and sauntered in Danny's direction.

"How's the shoulder?" he asked, smugly.

Danny resisted the urge to whack Tony and instead completely blanked him. He'd made up his mind to rise above any taunts and he wasn't going to be steered away from that path.

Tony clearly didn't like this ignoring act, and he muttered something else, but Danny just kept on walking. Today wasn't about verbal jousting; it was about driving. And whatever happened, Danny intended to drive the race of his life.

"Are you all right, mate?" asked Dad when Danny returned.

"I'm fine," replied Danny.

"The clerk of the race is an old mate of mine called Steve Cranshaw," said Alfie. "He just came round handing out the schedules for the race. You've got a three-lap practice at one forty-five p.m."

Danny hung out with Carl for a bit, went over his kart again to make some last-minute tweaks with Dad and then spent some time with Mum and Katie, who had just arrived.

Katie was beside herself with excitement both about the race and all of the action going on around her. She was talking at a thousand miles an hour and after a while Mum took her off to explore the rest of the site to give Danny some much-needed calmer time.

And then it was time to wheel the kart to the start of the track.

Danny spotted Tony Butler up ahead, wheeling his kart in the same direction with his dad.

When all fourteen semi-finalists were gathered, standing ready by their karts and trolleys, Steve Cranshaw appeared and introduced himself. "OK, everyone, there are fourteen of you in the Granger Cup Semi-Final and we'll be starting the race on the dot at two thirty p.m. – we've got to stick rigidly to the schedule as there are so many other races today. I want everyone to listen carefully."

Danny gulped nervously.

"You'll have three practice laps and on the basis of those and your times from the quarter-finals and other rounds of the competition, I'll be deciding your positions on the grid. I know this is a very big race for all of you and I wish you good luck. Are there any questions?"

There were none.

"Right, let's get going."

Danny was out quickly on the first practice lap. Having seen Alfie's footage of the track immediately proved incredibly useful. Danny already knew when to expect the straights and corners, and he was ready for the triple apex of Bend 7. Two laps later and he felt he had a good handle on the course. Knowing its exact layout had been a stroke of genius on Alfie's part and this knowledge helped to relax Danny, even if it was only a tiny bit. He hoped that with his track record to date in the Granger Cup rounds, his laps were good enough for Steve Cranshaw to give him a decent starting spot on the grid.

He drove back to the start/finish area in relatively good spirits. He climbed out and knelt down with Dad and Alfie to tighten a couple of bolts and make a slight adjustment to the seat straps. It wasn't long before Steve Cranshaw appeared again.

"Listen in!" he declared. He then proceeded to read out the starting positions. Danny was in sixth. Tony Butler was in fifth. They'd be side by side at the start. Great! Danny would be positioned right next to the kid who'd tried to mow him off the track in the quarters.

The Granger Cup karts were wheeled to the side of the starting grid as another group of drivers appeared for their heat; and then another; and another.

Nerves were biting at Danny and he tried to focus on the advice that Alfie and Dad were giving him. Carl was standing behind the fence giving him constant smiles of encouragement and thumbs ups. It made Danny feel a fraction better to know that the three of them plus Mum and Katie would all be trackside willing him to finish in one of the three qualifying spots.

"Granger Cup semi-finalists, take your places on the grid now!" declared Steve Cranshaw. For a split second Danny was revisited by all of his fears and doubts regarding the race and was overcome by a last-minute urge to leap over the fence and run away.

But Alfie's hand firmly clamped him on the shoulder (maybe Alfie could read his mind) and Dad wheeled Danny's kart on to the third line of two on the grid just as Tony Butler's dad was doing the same.

"Six laps!" shouted out Cranshaw. "I want good, clean, safe driving!"

With their karts in place, side by side on the starting grid, both Danny and Tony eased themselves into their respective vehicles and pulled on the seat straps.

Danny took an extremely deep breath and blew out his cheeks. *Think positive,* he ordered himself. *Think about what Scot Devlin said. If I carry on driving well, a sponsor will come to me – I just need to focus on my driving and block everything else out.*

But these positive thoughts were smashed to one side by the single word Tony Butler hissed sideways at him.

"Loser!"

Danny felt his insides go haywire. But he didn't even give Tony the benefit of a look. He simply blanked him again and ordered himself to get into the zone and focus only on himself and his own driving. He was going to drive this race on his terms, not on Tony's, and no amount of taunting would ruffle him – at least that was the plan.

"OK," said Alfie, kneeling down beside Danny's kart, as Steve Cranshaw held a quick discussion with a couple of race marshals who were wearing their distinctive fluorescent-yellow jackets. "You can do this – you really can. Think about everything we've discussed, look out for Bend 7 and focus on the third straight as your long overtaking lane. Got it?"

Danny nodded and pulled his helmet on.

All along the grid the other drivers followed suit, listening to the last-ditch advice their mentors were issuing.

"Whatever happens out there, you're still a brilliant driver," said Dad as Alfie moved away with a final pat on Danny's back.

"Thanks, Dad," replied Danny, his hands gripping the steering wheel tightly.

Mike Butler whispered something to Tony. They shook hands and Mike moved away.

"We're all behind you," smiled Dad, "just try your hardest!"

Danny and his father shook hands.

"Everyone is now ready for the race to start!" declared Steve Cranshaw.

"Go for it!" mouthed Dad, hurrying away with all of the other last-minute pep-talkers.

Steve Cranshaw checked his watch and looked at the race marshal, who was standing and holding a green flag by the side at the front of the grid. Cranshaw nodded at him, and with a smooth flowing movement the marshal waved the flag.

Fourteen karts surged forward.

One semi-final; six laps; three spots to bag a place in a national final.

The Granger Cup Semi was on!

Danny accelerated, feeling the roar of his kart and the other thirteen pounding the track. With the disadvantage in kart quality, he had to be completely tuned in to every aspect of his driving – steering, braking, accelerating – everything. On lap one, the kart's suspension and balance felt fine; the steering wheel was steadying the vehicle, the tyres were doing their job. Tony had eased a few metres ahead of him but that was fine. Danny was determined to keep this separation-distance and not slip further behind.

He'd felt the bumpier ground at Bends 3 and 4 in the practice laps but touching seventy miles per hour he could feel them a lot more. By the end of the first lap the starting positions were rigid; no one had gone for the big break yet, but it was only a matter of time.

Thirty metres into lap two, the seventh-placed kart tried to burn Danny up, but with an injection of acceleration Danny just managed to hold his opponent off, having to grab the inside to maintain this objective. He really didn't want to be conceding places at any stage in the races. Being in sixth gave him a chance – any further back and he could well be in trouble. By the finish of the second lap, Danny still held sixth with Tony very firmly in his sights. Up ahead, though, there'd been a change with the first kart (deep red side bars) and second kart (light green side bars and nose cone) swapping places.

On the second straight of lap three, Danny and Tony both overtook the fourth-placed kart (swirly brown pattern on side bars) placing Danny in fifth and Tony in fourth. This was definitely a step in the right direction but it wasn't good enough. Fifth place was as good as nowhere. On the final straight of the third lap Danny tried to blaze past Tony but Tony just held him off.

Danny was aware of the crowds surrounding the track and knew that Mum, Dad, Katie, Carl and Alfie would be out there screaming themselves hoarse. This made him feel supported but also anxious – he couldn't let them down.

Danny would have to pass Tony and the streamlined grey kart in third position to get into the final places. He was now haring round lap four, well aware that he couldn't leave things too late. He tried to overtake Tony again on the long, third straight, but Tony kept him at bay by swerving leftwards and rebuffing Danny. Seeing Tony maintain an edge was getting to Danny and he knew he had to contain his bitterness and anger or he'd never stand a chance. Danny tried to overtake on Bend 7 of lap four, choosing to go outside, but Tony anticipated this move and blocked him.

Danny yelled out in frustration. *I HAVE TO GET PAST HIM!*

His hands were clenched so tightly on the wheel he feared they'd have to be prised off at the end of the race.

The blood was rushing between his ears and his heart was playing some kind of ferocious speed ping-pong inside his chest, but still he pressed on, raw energy and adrenaline flowing through him.

But by the end of lap four, Tony still had the edge on him and to Danny's despair, Tony increased the distance between them by another five metres, making Danny yell out again.

Danny sped down the first straight of lap five, willing himself on, hoping for Tony to lose concentration, even for a second, to give Danny an overtaking opportunity. He tried again on Bend 4, but Tony just kept ahead.

And then the overtaking footage Alfie had shown him down at Sparks Cross a while ago suddenly flew into Danny's brain in glorious colour. The images of Formula One drivers picking their moments to perfection spun through his mind, and remembering everything he'd seen and talked about with Alfie, Danny gritted his teeth and the second he hit the third straight, he put every sinew, muscle and nerve into taking on Tony.

With a crescendo of engine noise and a rapid swing to the inside of the track, Danny emulated his Formula One heroes, picking the exact moment to finally pass Tony's kart with a sizzling burst of speed!

A massive burst of elation exploded inside him, but it was short-lived. Yes, he'd overtaken Tony and grabbed fourth place – but this still wasn't enough to snatch him a qualifying place. He had to make third or all of his efforts would be for dust.

In a flash it was lap six and Danny now faced the dual tasks of holding Tony off and getting past the grey in third. Danny tried going outside on Bend 4, but the grey stayed ahead, just.

Danny's whole body was clenched with tension and fear.

He had to take third!

But after curving round Bend 3, something completely unexpected happened. Just after hitting the second straight, smoke started wafting out from the engine of the third-placed grey kart. The driver panicked and skidded straight into Danny's path.

Danny shouted out and just managed to swerve round the kart, avoiding a massive collision but putting himself in third place. He took a quick look back, wanting to see if the lad in the smoking kart was OK. Three race marshals were already leaping over the barriers, racing towards the vehicle.

But in the split second Danny turned round, Tony Butler's kart overtook his.

NOOOOOOOOO!

In shock Danny tried to regain the advantage, but Tony had pulled a few metres ahead. How could he have been so stupid?

Furious with himself, Danny pushed his kart aggressively, biting at Tony's wheels, but Tony was equally determined and kept his slender advantage.

Danny knew that the third straight would be his last chance to beat Tony. And it wasn't long before this stretch of track loomed up.

Come on! I've overtaken Tony once, I can do it again!

Danny gave it everything; he smashed forward and drew level with Tony.

It has to be NOW!

But Tony pre-empted Danny's lunge on to the outside and mirrored his move, blocking his way.

Danny screamed in frustration.

He tried the inside but Tony blocked him again.

This is my last chance. It's now or never!

And then they were shooting across the finish line; Tony in third, Danny in fourth.

Tony had qualified for the Granger Cup Final.

Danny hadn't.

It was over.

Danny's utter despair was interrupted for a second when he saw that the driver of the smoking grey kart was completely fine. He heard someone shouting something about an electrical fault and that luckily a full-on fire had been prevented by the quick work of the marshals. He was happy for the lad.

But then the agony of losing closed in on Danny.

He yanked off his seat straps and ripped off his helmet, chucking it down on to the kart's seat. The last person in the whole world he wanted to see was standing in his way, a smile the size of a small country spread right across his face. Before Tony could even open his mouth to make a smug, gloating comment, Danny sidestepped him, jumped over a barrier and stomped off in the direction of the path leading out of Hardy Bridge.

He was so furious that he took absolutely no notice of the commotion that had erupted behind him. Who cared what anyone else was doing? He'd blown it BIG TIME! He should never have listened to Dad, Alfie and Scot Devlin. His instinct had been right; stay out of the race and avoid defeat. But he'd done it now. The race was over. It didn't matter that he came fourth; he may as well have finished fourteenth. All that mattered was that he hadn't qualified for the final and Tony Butler had. It was gut-wrenching and humiliating.

Tony would spread his victory over school. It would be a complete nightmare!

"Danny!" called Dad, hurrying after him. Danny was aware of some other shouting going on behind him but he wasn't interested.

"LEAVE ME ALONE!" shouted Danny, starting to run and not turning round.

"Danny!"

"I'M OUT OF HERE!"

Danny upped his pace and kept going.

"DANNY – YOU NEED TO GET BACK HERE NOW! MR CRANSHAW WANTS TO SEE YOU URGENTLY!"

Danny froze in his tracks. It must be about the fire. Steve Cranshaw was probably taking statements from drivers who'd been close to it. It was a bad idea to ignore a request from a race clerk, however angry and bitter you felt. His shoulders sagged. He turned round slowly.

He shuffled back towards Dad, who gave his shoulders a squeeze. "Come on, mate, hurry!"

As they walked back to the start/finish area, Danny

saw Tony Butler throw a wrench on the ground in apoplectic rage.

"NO WAY!" Tony was yelling in Mr Cranshaw's face. "YOU'VE GOT IT WRONG!" Cranshaw looked totally calm in the face of Tony's outburst.

Alfie was standing a few metres to the side of Tony, a very solemn look on his face.

Danny and Dad quickly walked over to Alfie.

"THAT'S A LIE!" screamed Tony at Cranshaw.

"What's going on?" demanded Danny.

"I heard Tony's kart making higher revs when he pulled off the grid," said Alfie. "It sounded like anti-heat had been illegally sprayed on the clutch of his kart. So I mentioned this to Steve Cranshaw and he's just checked it out; seems like Tony and his father haven't exactly played by the rules."

"DO SOMETHING, DAD!" wailed Tony.

"As I said, there's been a serious contravention of the rules," said Mr Cranshaw to the Butlers. "I need to see you both in the organizers' office in ten minutes, unless you want to conduct the judicial out here?"

Tony looked as if he was about to burst out crying. He

and his father stomped off under a cloud of rage and shame.

Steve Cranshaw swivelled on his heels and marched straight over to Danny.

"As clerk of this course today, I have made a judgement that the driver who finished third in the Granger Cup Semi-Final did so by cheating and has therefore been disqualified."

There were gasps all around from the other drivers, who by now had all finished the race and had climbed out of their karts.

Danny looked at Dad, then at Alfie, then at Carl, who'd walked over to join them.

"As the fourth-placed driver, Danny Sharp has gained third position in this race and has therefore qualified for the Granger Cup Final."

Danny, Dad, Alfie and Carl didn't react for a split second, but then the four of them threw their arms around each other and leapt in the air. Then Mum and Katie showed up and Dad broke away to explain to them what had happened. Mum gave Danny a huge hug and Katie leapt into his arms.

In the background, Tony Butler and his father could be heard exchanging furious insults.

But no one in Danny's party showed any interest. They were all talking at the same time; excited cries and shouts and chatter bouncing between them.

"Hang on a second. Hang on a SECOND!" commanded Dad suddenly. They all fell silent.

"It's fine to go a bit mad, but there are lots of other people around here who probably don't want to listen to our wild celebrations. I suggest we clock out with the organizers and go back home for a celebration meal. What do you say?"

"YES!" was the unanimous and joyful response.

Alfie put his arm round Danny's shoulders and gave him the widest of smiles.

"All wagons on the road then!" declared Dad. "We have a party to get to!"

Danny and Dad went to the organizers' hut to announce they were leaving the course. They received written confirmation of Danny's third-place finish and berth in the Granger Cup Final. Danny gripped the piece of paper as if his life depended on it. It was the most important document he'd ever handled and there was no way he was letting anyone else get their grubby hands on it!

Dad, Mum and Alfie drove back in convoy to the Sharps' house in their respective vehicles. In Dad's van, Danny and Carl sang and chanted the whole way home, with Dad joining in when he knew the words or somewhere near them. The second they reached the house, Dad went straight to the freezer, pulled out some pizzas and stuck them in the oven. Mum made a big salad. Danny and Carl set the kitchen table, while Katie ran everywhere chanting her older brother's name.

"Grub's up!" announced Dad, twenty minutes later.

Everyone tucked in hungrily, no one more so than Danny, who realized he hadn't eaten for hours.

"This is only the beginning!" cried Carl between mouthfuls of pizza. "First stop the Granger Cup Final, next stop the F1 Grand Prix Circuit!"

"Hear, hear!" chipped in Alfie.

"I think. . ." tried Dad, but Danny got there first.

"I know, we shouldn't get our hopes up!"

This produced gunfire blasts of laughter from everyone but Dad, who asked, "Am I that easy to read?"

"Yes!" laughed Mum. "Now who's for ice cream?"

Danny soaked up the jokes and laughter and savoured the fantastic mood. He was delighted to have made the final for himself, but he was also thrilled for the others. They, after all, were the ones who had put up with his bad moods, his self-doubt and his gripes – and there'd been plenty of them recently. He was also flooded with relief that he'd taken Scot Devlin's advice and gone ahead with the race – he *would* have regretted it hugely if he'd missed it.

An hour later, when Mum was mooting the idea of Katie going up to bed and Katie was fighting against this plan, the front doorbell rang.

Danny's heart suddenly leapt.

Maybe Scot Devlin heard I made the final?

"I'll get it," said Dad, standing up.

"No, it's mine," cut in Danny, quickly edging past his father.

He hurried out of the kitchen and down the corridor, reached for the front door handle and yanked it open.

But it wasn't Scot Devlin on the doorstep.

It was Frank Hoult.

"M . . . Mr Hoult," stammered Danny in surprise, "what are you doing here? Sorry, I mean, come in."

"Thank you," nodded Mr Hoult, stepping inside.

"Er . . . we're all in the kitchen," explained Danny in confusion, leading him towards the others.

All conversation immediately ceased when Danny ushered the guest into the kitchen.

Dad, as the only other person who knew Mr Hoult, stood up, looking very shocked, and announced, "This is Frank Hoult, the managing director of Point Power Electronics. Mr Hoult, this is my wife, Julie, and this is Alfie Price – manager of Sparks Cross. This is Danny's best friend, Carl, and this is our daughter, Katie.""

Looks criss-crossed around the room and puzzled faces were pulled.

"Please sit down," offered Dad.

Mr Hoult pulled up a chair and squeezed in between Dad and Katie.

"It's very kind of you to let me in," started Mr Hoult, "especially after what I'm sure must have been the heartache of our phone call on Friday night."

Everyone round the table nodded silently.

"On Friday before I phoned you," went on Mr Hoult, "myself and our team of senior managers took a vote about whether or not to sponsor you. It was five against four to not go ahead and I thought that was that. But then I spoke to you, Mrs Sharp."

He turned to face Mum. "Your words resonated in my mind," he continued, "the things you said show how much you and Mr Sharp *believe* in Danny's abilities, and not just because you're his parents."

"You're a hundred per cent right about that," nodded Dad, "we really think he's got what it takes to go somewhere in the sport. I mean, you should have seen him in the race today – against the odds, he qualified for the Granger Cup Final; you can't ask better than that."

"I know," nodded Mr Hoult, "I was at Hardy Bridge today."

There was a collective intake of breath – this was totally unexpected.

"Sorry, Mr Hoult," said Mum with a bewildered look on her face, "you came to watch Danny even though you'd decided not to sponsor him?"

"After my phone call with you on Friday night, I rang round my team and said that although I respected the result of the vote we took, I'd like them to keep a final decision about this matter on hold. I told them I wanted to see you drive again before I totally closed the page and I managed to convince two of them to come with me today – two of the five who voted against sponsoring you."

Alfie, Mum and Dad were staring at Mr Hoult with an intensity that was almost frightening. Carl was playing with his spoon and looking spellbound. Katie looked as if she was about to cry.

"These two colleagues had never been to watch karting before, and as well as loving the whole occasion, they were completely blown away by Danny's driving."

Danny had the feeling that something was about to happen that would rock the very foundations of his world.

"So what happens now?" asked Dad edgily.

"Y . . . you don't mean that you're going to. . ." uttered Danny in astonishment.

"I'm here," said Mr Hoult with a very broad smile, "because my two colleagues changed their minds after watching Danny today, and that swings the vote firmly in Danny's favour. I'm here because I want to formally offer Danny a sponsorship deal with Point Power Electronics – and I want to offer him such a deal before another company swoops in and signs him up!"

"Incredible!" mouthed Alfie.

Carl punched the air.

"You're serious?" asked Dad, little lamps of excitement and joy burning in his eyes.

"Absolutely!" nodded Mr Hoult. "I'm sorry for any upset I've caused and I'm hoping you'll forgive me about the initial rejection. I would be very delighted, as would my colleagues, if you would accept my offer. Of course there'll be quite a lot of specifics to hammer out, paperwork to be drawn up and contracts to sign, but I really think my company can offer you a fantastic and highly promising relationship. Having seen your performance today, I truly believe you've got what it takes to go all the way! What do you say, Danny?"

What did he say?

Danny Sharp stood up and reached over the table to give Mr Hoult a very firm handshake.

"I take it that's a yes?" laughed Mr Hoult.

Danny nodded his head vigorously.

Formula One – just watch out!

Jonny Zucker worked as a teacher and stand-up comedian before turning to writing full-time. He has now written over thirty books for children, teenagers and adults. Jonny became a fan of Formula One at a young age and first drove a kart at the age of eight. Jonny has always wanted to bring the excitement and nail-biting tension of racing to readers, and is pleased he can do this through Danny Sharp. Jonny lives with his wife and three young children in North London.

Read Danny Sharp's first adventure

"If you like Formula One, you'll love this"
David Coulthard

SPEED MACHINE

Jonny Zucker

*Karting means everything to Danny.
One day he hopes he'll even be a
Formula One champion.*

*But someone is willing to go to any lengths
to sabotage Danny's chances in the race.*

Can Danny defeat his rivals?